CW00339524

Sharpshooters in the Hills

Two sharpshooters, McGee and Salmon, go into Indian territory hoping to claim a reward. First they must find a man named Roger Stone, who has disappeared in the Black Hills but death dogs their progress. Stone had already been murdered and McGee is attacked by an Indian. Salmon is close to being hanged.

Their friend, Dan the whiskey man and his daughter, Daisy, turn up in Caraton. He has a mysterious order to supply one hundred bottles of whiskey.

Will they inflame the Indians' brooding resentment at being herded into the reservation? Will the duo be able to stop the proposed uprising? They will need all their sharpshooting skills to survive the gun battles ahead.

Sharpshooters in the Hills

Ron Watkins

A Black Horse Western

ROBERT HALE · LONDON

© Ron Watkins 2009
First published in Great Britain 2009

ISBN 978-0-7090-8692-5

Robert Hale Limited
Clerkenwell House
Clerkenwell Green
London EC1R 0HT

www.halebooks.com

Typeset by
Derek Doyle & Associates, Shaw Heath
Printed and bound in Great Britain by
CPI Antony Rowe, Wiltshire

CHAPTER 1

McGee was studying the *Stoneville Gazette.*

'I don't know why you buy that paper every week,' said Salmon. 'There's never anything interesting in it.'

'That's where you're wrong,' retorted McGee. 'It's full of interesting pieces of information.'

'Find me one,' came the reply.

The two were seated on the veranda of their house. In it lived McGee and his wife, Letitia, together with Salmon and his wife, Jill. In addition there were two young offspring – Sam, who was McGee's and Letitia's son and Rose, who was Salmon's and Jill's daughter.

'Don't you feel that we should be doing better than this?' replied McGee. He waved an apologetic hand at the house behind them.

'It's home,' said Salmon, defensively. 'Anyhow Jill and Letitia like it.'

'They like it because they like Stoneville. It's got everything they need. Mothers' meetings. Young adults' classes. Who the hell invented the phrase, young adults? Our children are only two years old, for God's sake.'

Salmon ignored him and rolled a cigarette. He knew that McGee was in – what he termed – one of his moods. It consisted of his friend arguing against everything and everybody in sight. These black moods came on every few months. During the years Salmon had learned to ignore them.

'Have a smoke,' he said, handing McGee his pouch of tobacco. But McGee's attention was directed once again at the newspaper and he ignored the offer.

'This isn't a bad place to live,' stated Salmon. 'We ride the range but we don't work too hard. We make enough money to live comfortably—

'Twenty dollars a week,' said McGee, scornfully. 'We could be earning that every night if we were back in New York.'

'And whose fault is it that we had to leave New York? Who ended up owing Charlie the Hook five thousand dollars,' said Salmon, stung at last into making a reply to McGee's complaints.

'Yeah, I know. It was all my fault,' said a slightly contrite McGee.

'We haven't got the pressure of preparing for a show,' Salmon pointed out. He had been the strong man and sharpshooter in the circus they worked for in New York. McGee had also been a sharpshooter.

McGee had turned his attention to the newspaper. 'A thousand dollars,' he said, half to himself. 'What could we do with a thousand dollars?'

'What are you talking about?' demanded Salmon.

McGee pointed to an article in the paper. 'It says here that the government is offering a thousand dollars.'

'What for?'

'Finding a man.'

'Have they lost the president?'

'Very funny,' retorted McGee. 'The man is somebody who makes maps.'

This time Salmon was genuinely puzzled. 'Why should they offer all that money to find a man who makes maps?'

'Well, there is a slight snag.'

'What is it?'

'He's got lost in the Black Hills.'

'There's no way that we're going to look for him,' said Salmon, emphatically.

'Think of it. Five hundred dollars each,' said McGee, dreamily.

'I'm not thinking about it. Neither are you,' said Salmon, positively. 'People get killed when they go there,' he went on. 'Look what happened to Custer.'

7

'That was over ten years ago. Things have settled down now.'

'We'd still be going into Indian Territory.'

McGee didn't miss the fact that Salmon was partly considering the idea. 'They're all living on the reservation. All we'd have to do is to go there and find this guy. And pocket a thousand dollars. Think of it. You'd be able to give Jill enough money to buy some nice new clothes for herself. And for Rose.'

Salmon considered it for a few moments. 'The answer is still no,' he said at last.

'You said that we could do with some new furniture. With the money we'd bring back here there'd be no problem in buying some.'

This time the pause was longer. McGee sensed that he was winning. 'I've got fifty dollars I've saved up. I was going to use it in the next poker game in town. But half of it is yours to give to Jill. I'll give the other half to Letitia. It should be enough to keep them in food until we come back. We should only be away a couple of weeks at the most.'

'How far away are the Black Hills?' demanded Salmon.

McGee knew that he had won.

'About five days' ride,' he announced.

CHAPTER 2

In fact it took them seven days. Their first sight of the hills was the snow-capped peaks in the distance.

'He could be anywhere up in those mountains,' groaned Salmon. 'We've come on a wild-goose chase.'

'We'll go to the Army camp and see what they've got to say,' stated McGee.

The army camp consisted of several low sheds. The largest of them was in the centre. The camp was guarded by a barbed-wire fence. There were two guards at the entrance.

One of them stepped in front of McGee.

'You'll have to state your business before you can go in.'

'We're just travelling through, Sergeant,' said McGee.

The soldier studied them. 'Are you on official business?'

9

'You could say that. We're looking for the guy who's lost. The map-maker.'

'Right. You'd better go in.'

They entered a small office. It was sparsely furnished. A captain was sitting behind a desk. He waved them to the two chairs on the other side of the desk.

'What can I do for you, gentlemen?'

'My name is McGee and this is my friend, Salmon. We've come here to search for the map-maker.'

The captain, who had spent at least twenty years rising through the ranks, stared at them with an expressionless face.

'I don't think I can help you,' he said. 'Mr Stone called here about three months ago. He said he was going into the Black Hills to draw some maps. I told him I didn't think that was a wise thing to do. He said he had been appointed by the United States Government. There was nothing I could say to make him change his mind. And off he went.'

'Into the Black Hills?' ventured Salmon.

'That's right. We don't know how high they are, since they haven't been mapped. But there's snow on the top of them all the year round. If I may say so you two don't look prepared to go into the hills.'

'Why not?' demanded McGee.

'It's cold up there. Even though it's summer. You

10

want to get some warmer clothes if you're really thinking of going after him.'

'In that case maybe we'd better forget about the whole scheme,' said a resigned Salmon.

'Is there a store around where we can buy warmer clothes?' asked McGee.

'Sure. There's a store in the camp.'

At the entrance to the store they were again stopped by two guards.

'Will you state your business?' demanded one.

McGee explained that they had been to see the captain in the office. He had advised them to see about getting some warm clothing since they intended going into the Black Hills.

'Did he also tell you to make sure that you made your will?' said one soldier. The other laughed uproariously.

McGee scowled. 'It can't be all that dangerous, can it?'

'We can look after ourselves,' stated Salmon, positively.

'You might be able to, but I wouldn't fancy the chances of the little guy here.'

McGee looked around. There was a line that had been erected a few yards inside the camp. On it some battered tins had been placed. It was obvious that they had been used for target practice by some of the soldiers.

'Do you fancy putting your money where your

11

mouth is,' snapped McGee. 'I'll bet you ten dollars I can hit more of the tins at thirty paces than you can.'

The soldier who had laughed at his companion's description of McGee thought he had spotted an easy way to make some money.

'I've got ten dollars here that says my friend can hit more cans than you can.'

'I've got ten,' said the first soldier.

'Right. So it's a twenty-dollar bet,' said McGee.

Salmon took off his hat. He placed their last twenty dollars into the hat. The two soldiers put their contribution in.

'Six shots to start with,' said McGee. 'The first one to miss a can is the loser.'

'Yes, that's all right with me.' The soldier counted out thirty paces. He stopped opposite the cans. 'When your friend says the word, I'll shoot.'

'One, two, three. Fire,' said Salmon.

The soldier took deliberate aim. He fired at the first can and hit it. He continued to aim at the others. He hit numbers two, three and four. But he missed five.

'Blast,' he said with annoyance. 'I've shot four. Let's see if you can do better.'

McGee took up his position opposite the cans. Whereas the soldier had aimed carefully before shooting. McGee's gun was in his holster.

'When are you going to start shooting?' asked the soldier.

'Now!' replied McGee. He drew his revolver so quickly that the movement was just a blur. He fired six shots in rapid succession hitting a can every time.

The soldiers stared, open-mouthed at the feat. When they had recovered from their surprise the first one said, 'That was great shooting.'

'For a little guy?' asked McGee, drily.

'I'm sorry about that remark.'

'We don't mind paying up in order to see that kind of shooting,' said the other.

'We want to see about getting a few extra blankets and things,' said Salmon.

'You'll find all you'll need inside the store,' said the soldier.

CHAPTER 3

The duo's soldier friends had told them that the Indian reservation was a couple of miles along the trail. They found it easily since there were dozens of tepees in the enclosure.

There was no barbed wire around the reservation, but there were a couple of braves guarding the entrance. They were fine specimens of men who were stripped to the waist.

'You'd think they'd find it cold dressed like that,' observed Salmon.

'No white men allowed on Indian reservation,' said one.

'You speak English,' said a surprised McGee.

'No white men allowed on Indian reservation,' repeated the Indian.

'We get the picture,' stated McGee. 'We're look-

14

ing for a white man.'

The Indian gave an expressive shrug.

'Where do we go from here?' demanded Salmon.

The answer came in the form of a white woman who had stepped out of one of the nearby tepees.

'Can I help you?' she demanded.

'I hope so,' replied McGee. 'We're looking for the map-maker, Roger Stone.'

'You'd better come in.' She spoke to the guards in an Indian tongue. It was obviously about giving McGee and Salmon permission to enter the reservation, since one Indian gave an expressive shrug and waved them through.

'This is my tepee,' said their guide. 'I'm afraid you'll have to sit on the floor.'

'Let me introduce ourselves,' said McGee. 'This is Salmon and I'm McGee.'

When they were seated they studied one another. McGee had already observed that the lady was pretty, probably in her late twenties and not wearing a wedding ring. Salmon, who was less observant, waited for the lady to introduce herself.

'I'm Sister Amy,' she said.

'You're a religious sister?' asked a surprised McGee.

'That's right,' she smiled. 'There are six of us ladies here altogether. The government wants to try to convert as many Indians to Christianity as possible. They probably think that if they become Christians then they will stop fighting us.'

'But isn't it dangerous for young women to live here among the Indians?' demanded McGee.

'We thought it might be. But we've been here for three months, and anyhow we've got somebody looking after us.'

'Who's that?' demanded Salmon.

'Why, the Lord, of course. Anyhow that's enough about us. What about you two? When was the last time you had a meal.'

'Yesterday,' replied Salmon.

'Right, I'll arrange something.' She stood up. 'I'm afraid I can't say make yourselves comfortable while I'm away.' She gave them a smile before leaving the tepee.

'She's a lovely lady,' said Salmon.

'Yes.' McGee nodded in agreement.

'You keep your eyes off her,' said Salmon, warningly.

'What do you mean?' demanded McGee, innocently.

'You know what I mean. You've got a one-track mind. If you see a pretty lady in a skirt you can't resist the temptation. Especially if Letitia isn't around.'

'Nonsense,' stated McGee. 'Anyhow, she's married already.'

16

'I didn't see a wedding ring,' answered Salmon.

'To God,' said McGee, impatiently. 'That's what these religious women claim.'

They were stopped from further discussion by the arrival of Amy. She was followed by an Indian girl who was carrying a tray. Amy said something to the Indian who put the tray down on the floor.

'This is Petra,' said Amy. 'She's become a Christian. She's learning English.'

Petra flashed McGee a smile. 'I am learning – slowly,' she said.

'If we're here for any time, I'll be pleased to help you,' stated McGee.

Petra flashed him another smile before leaving the tepee.

'Help yourselves to the food,' said Amy, pointing to the two bowls on the plate. 'I'm afraid most of it is rabbit. But you'll find it quite tasty.'

'It looks delicious,' said Salmon.

'Now, if you'll excuse me, I've got to make arrangements for the evening service.' She left the tent and the duo gratefully tucked into their meal.

About twenty minutes later McGee and Salmon had finished their meal and were smoking the small cigars they had brought with them. Amy entered.

'That was a lovely meal,' said Salmon. 'It's the best meal we've had since we started out.'

17

'I hope you don't mind us smoking in your tent,' said McGee.

'Not at all. In fact there's one favour you can do for me.'

'What's that?'

'Could you give me one of your cigars. That's the one thing I miss on the reservation – a good smoke.'

McGee gave her a cigar and she lit it carefully. After inhaling the first drag she sighed contentedly.

'Ah, that's lovely.'

'Isn't it rather unusual? For a religious woman to be smoking?' ventured Salmon.

'Not at all. It's got nothing against smoking in the Bible. If tobacco had been discovered before Christ was born, I bet some of the disciples would have been smokers.' After taking another couple of puffs, she said: 'I assume you two will be staying the night.'

'If it's convenient,' said McGee.

'There's no problem. I've found an empty tepee for you. There is one thing though.'

'What's that?' demanded Salmon.

'You'll be expected to come to the evening service. I hold an evening service every evening about an hour before sunset.'

'We'll be there,' promised McGee. 'And I'll bring this choirboy with me.'

18

Amy smiled. 'Salmon a choirboy? Somehow I can't imagine it.'

'I was very young at the time,' Salmon announced.

CHAPTER 4

The service was held in the open air. Salmon and McGee were introduced to the five other evangelists. There were two who were older than the others: they were probably in their forties. Amy introduced them as Lizzie and Alice. There was Emma, she was obviously the youngster of the group – in fact hardly more than a teenager. She was quite attractive with long black hair framing a pretty oval face. Then there was Beth. She was as plain as Emma was pretty. Last of all came Flora. She hadn't been given a very apt name, thought McGee. She was definitely not like any flower that he could name. In fact she was manly in appearance with a deep voice to match.

Flora's deep voice came in handy when the service came to the hymn singing. In fact her singing and Salmon's were the highlight of the short service. Many of the Indians were standing around watching the service. The only one who took part, however, was Petra.

McGee approached Amy after the service.

'It was a nice service. It's a pity that some of the Indians didn't join in.'

'They're still antagonistic to us after what we did to them. They'll come round in time,' she said with a smile.

'Do you believe that?' McGee asked Salmon as they were walking back to their tepee.

Salmon checked that they were out of earshot of Amy. 'No,' he replied.'

'The Indians who were standing around are the most miserable-looking specimens of humanity I've seen outside a prison,' said McGee.

'I wouldn't trust any of them,' voiced Salmon.

'Did you see the way some of them were looking at Amy and the others.'

'What do you mean?'

'They were lusting after them.'

'How do you know?'

'Because I share the same feelings when I see a pretty girl. It takes one to know one.'

'Are you sure?'

'Of course I'm sure. If I were Sister Amy I'd pack up my tambourine and go home tomorrow.'

When they were back in their tent Amy put in an appearance. She joined them, sitting cross-legged on the floor.

'I'm sorry the service wasn't a great success,' she said. 'Oh, I've said that already, haven't I?' she added, with a smile.

'McGee says that he wouldn't trust them an inch. Especially after the way some of them were looking at you and the others,' said Salmon.

Amy glanced at McGee. 'I take it you're an expert on lust,' she said coldly.

'I've had my moments,' replied McGee.

'I'm sorry. I shouldn't have made that remark. It was out of order. I apologize.'

'There's no need. I think we should have a frank discussion. What I saw on the faces of the Indians can be summed up in a four-letter word – and I don't mean love.'

Amy sighed. 'Can I have another one of your cigars, please?'

When the three of them had lit up, Amy began: 'You won't understand this. But we feel that we're doing the Lord's work. We feel that we have been called here to preach the gospel. We call ourselves the Children of God. We feel that the Lord will look after us. And anyhow, there are nearly a hundred soldiers a couple of miles along the trail,' she added, with a smile.

When they had finished their cigars, Amy asked: 'When are you thinking of moving on?'

Salmon shrugged and glanced at McGee. 'We'll stay for a couple of days. The horses could do with a rest. And there a few things we've got to sort out before we go up into the mountains.'

'Right. I'll see you in morning. God be with you,' she said, as she left the tent.

Shortly afterwards the two settled down for the night.

'I never thought I'd ever be spending the night with a couple of hundred Indians,' said McGee.

Salmon's reply was a loud snore.

CHAPTER 5

Some time in the middle of the night the peace of the camp was shattered by an unearthly scream. The two men jumped out of their blankets and rushed out of the tent.

'Where did it come from?' demanded Salmon.

'I think it came from the tent that Emma is sharing with Sister Amy.' McGee was already heading for it.

It was a clear, starry night and they had no difficulty in distinguishing the tent. They also had no difficulty in distinguishing the Indian who came out of the tent furtively.

McGee was nearer the tent than Salmon.

'Stop!' he commanded.

The Indian turned. He saw the two white men and although he was at least thirty yards away, he drew a knife and flung it at McGee. It caught McGee in the shoulder. But not before McGee had been able to draw his revolver and fire. Testimony to the accuracy of McGee's shot was shown in the way the Indian collapsed on the ground.

'Is he dead?' demanded Salmon.

'Never mind about asking stupid questions. Get this knife out of my arm,' gritted McGee.

The other evangelists appeared. They, too, were starting to give vent to questions. These suddenly stopped when they noticed the blood that was spreading over McGee's shirt.

'This is going to hurt,' said Salmon.

'Get on with it,' said McGee, who was now lying on the ground.

Salmon seized the knife and with one pull drew it out from McGee's shoulder. For the second time that night a scream shattered the night air. This time it was McGee's.

'He's passed out,' said one of the evangelists.

'Bring him to my tent,' said Flora.

Salmon carried him to the tent and deposited him on a pile of furs.

'I've got to stop the blood,' said Flora. 'Take these petticoats and start ripping them up.' She handed a few petticoats to Salmon, who started carrying out her command.

Outside Amy had appeared from her tent. She was holding her hand to her head.

'What happened?' demanded Lizzie.

'One of the Indians came into our tent. Before

I knew what was happening he had hit me over the head.'

'He attacked you?' demanded Alice.

'Don't be stupid. He attacked Emma.'

'Is she—' demanded Lizzie.

'No. I asked her what happened. She said she struggled. He had put his hand over her mouth but she bit it. When he took his hand away, she screamed.'

'McGee shot him,' said Lizzie. 'But not before he had thrown a knife at McGee and hit him in the shoulder.'

'Where's McGee now?'

'Flora is looking after him.'

'I'll go and see to him.' She disappeared into Flora's tent.

There was the sound of horses galloping towards the camp. In a few moments a couple of soldiers appeared. They drew up in a cloud of dust.

'We heard shooting,' said one.

'It was my friend, McGee,' said Salmon, who had emerged from Flora's tent. 'He shot an Indian who was attacking a young lady. The Indian managed to throw a knife at him and it stuck in McGee's shoulder.'

'I'll go and fetch the doctor,' said one of the soldiers. He swung his horse in a tight turn and started to gallop back to the camp.

26

Flora, in the meantime, had lit a lamp.

'I hope the doctor brings some whiskey,' she said.

'Do you want a drink?' demanded Salmon.

'To clean the wound,' she said, impatiently.

The doctor made good time in coming to the reservation. He handed his horse to Salmon and went inside the tent.

'Has the wound been cleaned?' he demanded.

'We haven't any whiskey,' replied Flora.

The doctor produced a bottle and, having removed the petticoat pad, poured some gently on to the wound. McGee groaned as the spirit hit the raw flesh.

'It's a good thing the knife didn't go in too deep,' said the doctor.

'Is there anything we can do?' demanded Salmon.

'Not really,' said the doctor, who was bandaging the wound. 'I suppose you could pray.'

'We do that already,' said Flora.

'You mean – he's in danger – of dying?' Salmon choked on his words.

'With a wound like this you can never tell,' replied the doctor. 'The main thing is to keep him warm.'

Emma had entered the tent.

'I'll get some more buffalo skins.'

'You can't put too many on him. They'll press

down on the wound and stop it from knitting. He might become delirious in a few hours' time. As I said, try to keep him warm.' With those last words of advice the doctor left, after promising to come back in the morning.

'I'll look after him,' said Emma. 'After all, it's because of me that he's like this.'

'I'll call back in the morning,' said Salmon, as he left the tent.

'Don't forget to pray,' was Flora's parting shot.

'As I said, I'll look after him,' said Emma. 'You can go and take my bed in Lizzie's tent.

'Where are you going to sleep?' demanded Flora.

Emma's answer was to get into bed with McGee.

'This is the best method I know of keeping him warm,' she said, as she snuggled up close to him.

'I don't think our religion would sanction it,' said Flora. 'But in the circumstances I think it's the right thing to do.'

CHAPTER 6

Salmon woke early in the morning and went over to Flora's tent. He was surprised to find that Emma was there and not Flora. He was even more surprised to find that she was in bed with McGee.

They were both asleep and Salmon crept quietly out of the tent in order not to disturb them. Amy was approaching the tent and Salmon explained the situation to her.

'I know. Flora slept in my tent last night. She told me about Emma's decision to sleep with McGee to make sure that he doesn't become cold.'

'It's all right at the moment because he's unconscious. But when he recovers and finds a young lady in bed with him, the situation could change.'

'We'll cross that bridge when we come to it,' said Amy. 'I assume you want breakfast?'

'Yes, I could do with some chow.'

'I'll send Petra to your tent with some.'

Ten minutes later Petra appeared in Salmon's tent. She had a bowl on a tray. In it was a collection of unusual-looking herbs, together with pieces of meat.

'Eat,' she said. 'Very tasty.'

To Salmon's surprise the concoction was indeed tasty.

'You want I should go?' demanded Petra.

'No. Stay until I've finished. I want to ask you some questions.'

When he had finished his meal he reached for one of his cigars. Petra watched him with large brown eyes.

'What sort of Indian are you?'

'Cheyenne.'

'Your people fought against General Custer.'

'Yes. And the Sioux.'

She obviously knew more English than he had thought. He nodded appreciatively.

'Do you know why I'm here?'

'You're looking for a man. McGee too,' she added.

'Did Mr Stone ever come to the reservation?'

She nodded.

'You saw him?'

Another nod.

'Do you know how long ago that was?'

'Two – three moons.'

Two to three months, thought Salmon.

30

'Did he stay long?'

She obviously didn't understand the question. He tried another tack.

'This – Mr Stone's – tent?'

'Yes.'

'He stayed here?' Salmon held up his hand showing five fingers.

Petra shook her head.

Salmon held up both hands showing ten fingers. Petra nodded.

'Right. So we're getting somewhere,' said Salmon to himself. He tried another question. 'When he went away,' he did an impersonation of somebody riding a horse, which made Petra laugh, 'did he go up into the Black Hills?'

She stopped laughing long enough to shake her head.

A puzzled Salmon stared at her. 'Which way did he go?'

'To Caraton.'

'Caraton?' He had vaguely heard of it. It was the gold town that had sprung up twenty years ago when the gold rush up to the Black Hills had started.

'Why did he go to Caraton since he came here to draw maps?' he said, half to himself.

Petra rightly assumed that it was a rhetorical question and didn't try to answer it.

Salmon thought of another question. He did his

31

impersonation of somebody riding a horse. One again it sent Petra into peals of laughter.

'How far is Caraton?' He held up five fingers. Petra shook her head. He held up another five. She nodded.

At that moment Amy entered the tent.

'I hear you are keeping Petra amused,' she said. 'She has a very infectious laugh.'

Petra assumed it was time for her to leave. With a smile towards Salmon she picked up the tray and left.

'She was telling me about Roger Stone,' said Salmon. 'She said that when he left here he went to Caraton. I would have thought he would have headed up into the Black Hills.'

'Maybe he wanted some extra supplies,' she suggested.

'Yeah. Maybe,' agreed Salmon. 'By the way, can I offer you a cigar?'

'No, thanks. It's a bit too early in the morning for me. I'll have one later though if I may. At the moment I have to do what I call my penance.'

'What does that consist of?'

'I'm teaching a couple of dozen of the Indian children to sing a hymn. If you hear an unearthly din during the next half-hour, you'll know what it is.'

She stood up to go.

'Is there any news about McGee?'

'Not a lot. The doctor has been to see him. He says the fact that he is still sleeping is a good sign. He's given Emma some laudanam to give him when he wakes up.'

Salmon came to a decision. 'There isn't much point in me staying around here. I'm going into Caraton. There are some supplies we want, too.'

When he was saddling his horse, he heard the unearthly sound that Sister Amy had talked about. Through it he could just about distinguish Emma singing.

We have decided to follow Jesus.
We have decided to follow Jesus.
We have decided to follow Jesus,
No turning back. No turning back.

Would she ever convert any? he wondered. Still, they had converted Petra. That was an achievement, he mused, as he swung his horse towards Caraton.

CHAPTER 7

Salmon rode into Caraton at around midday. Everywhere there were signs proclaiming the town's connection with the gold rush of the past. He chose a saloon named The Golden Lode Saloon.

He ordered a steak and a beer. Steak was something he had missed while he had been on the road with McGee. When it came it proved to be succulent and he tucked into it with gusto.

He was seated in a part of the bar which was reserved for diners. When he had finished he moved to the main section where there were several card schools in progress. If McGee were with him now he wouldn't hesitate – he'd soon join one of the schools. However, card-playing – and particularly gambling – wasn't one of Salmon's vices. He sipped his beer as he idly watched one of the group of players.

At one of the tables, instead of a card school, half a dozen cowboys were indulging in arm wrestling. One of them, a large man, seemed to be winning every time he challenged one of the others. The rules of the game seemed to be that the two contestants put a dollar into the pot. They would wrestle until the one forced the other's arm down on to the table.

Suddenly one of the cowboys turned to him.

'Do you fancy your chances, big feller?'

Salmon hadn't intended joining in the game, but seeing the expectant faces round the table, he changed his mind.

'Why not?'

The large cowboy who had been winning every time said: 'There are new rules. We put five dollars into the pot. The winner takes it.'

If Salmon lost it would mean that it wouldn't leave him much money to spare. But looking at the expectant faces made him come to a decision.

'Right. I'll take the bet.'

He took up his position opposite the big cowboy.

'By the way, my name's Drake,' said the cowboy.

'I'm Salmon,' came the reply, as he adjusted his position slightly in order not to give the cowboy any advantage.

They grasped hands and the struggle began. Arm wrestling between two fairly equally matched rivals usually took several minutes. This was no exception. The cowboy was no easy opponent. Both men strained to get the important first advantage. Once that was achieved, even though the movement of the other's arm was slight, the advantage could be maintained.

Several others who had been standing by the bar came across to witness the struggle. The sweat was standing out on the foreheads of the two contestants. The cowboy bared his lips in an ugly grin as he struggled to gain an advantage.

Salmon's sojourn with the circus stood him in good stead. Part of his act had been to bend iron bars. Even though he had quit the circus a year or so ago, he still kept in training. On the ranch where he and McGee worked there were several old cannon balls, which had probably been left over from the Indian wars. Salmon had taken them to the local blacksmith and asked him if he could join two of them with a bar. The blacksmith had obliged with the result that Salmon had two perfect dumbbells that he used to train with on most days. McGee had often taunted him for his passion to keep in training.

'We'll never get another job in the circus,' he had scoffed. 'So there's no point in keeping fit.'

But it was at times like this that Salmon's daily exercises proved their worth. He realized after a couple of minutes that he was gaining the upper hand. To any of the dozen or so watchers there was no apparent change in their position. Both men were straining every sinew to force the other's hand down on to the table. But Salmon knew from the grimace on his opponent's face, which had changed with the pain that was now stamped on it, that he was slowly winning.

The question was how much longer would his opponent hold out? Salmon knew that at all costs he mustn't lose concentration. The danger was that, in knowing he was winning he could lose concentration and in that second the tables could be turned. He could find that he was losing instead of winning.

The first sign to the onlookers that the tide was turning in Salmon's favour came when the two hands which had held their upright position for several minutes began to show signs of movement. Salmon's hand began to push the cowboy's hand down. At first the movement was less than an inch at a time. But it gradually became more perceptible. The cowboy's hand was slowly moving towards the table and the moment of his eventual capitulation as Salmon kept on applying the pressure.

In fact the end of the contest came quite suddenly. One moment their hands were poised above the table at an angle instead of being upright. The next moment the cowboy gave a groan as his hand was forced down to lie flat under Salmon's hand.

To Salmon's surprise the watchers gave a round of applause.

'That was the best arm wrestling I've seen for some time,' said one.

The barman came across.

'Here's a free beer on the house,' he said, handing Salmon and the cowboy a glass each.

'I could do with this,' said Salmon.

It brought a grudging smile in response from the cowboy.

While they were sipping their beer, Salmon said: 'I wouldn't want too many of those contests.'

'You're the first one who's beaten me in arm wrestling,' confessed Drake.

'I used to be a strong man in a circus,' said Salmon. 'Maybe it was an advantage.'

'Which circus?' demanded Drake. 'It is around here?'

'No, in New York.'

'A pity,' said Drake. 'I wouldn't mind joining a circus. Do you think I would be suitable?'

'You'd have no problem. Just keep on training.'

Drake sipped his beer thoughtfully. 'But you've given it up now?'

'Yes. We've actually come here to try to find the guy who was lost – Roger Stone.'

Drake finished his beer.

'I don't envy you. There are three people who've tried to find him already. They all ended up dead.'

Salmon accepted the information with surprise.

'Dead?'

'It's all in the *Caraton Gazette*.' He stood up. 'Well good luck, anyhow. I won't shake hands. I don't think my hand has recovered yet from the beating it had.'

CHAPTER 8

Salmon mulled over the news he had received from Drake as he wandered down Main Street. Three people searching for Stone and ending up dead could only mean one thing. There was more danger attached to their mission than they had expected.

In fact, to be honest, the thought of danger had never entered their heads. They had assumed that they would go into the Black Hills. Maybe they would find Stone, or maybe they wouldn't. But to end up in Boot Hill had never entered his head. And he was sure it hadn't occurred to McGee either.

His thoughts were interrupted by the fact that he had just come as far as the *Caraton Gazette* office. It was blazoned over the front door of a large, low building. Although it had a front window it had been painted over with whitewash which prevented passers-by seeing inside.

Salmon knocked on the door and entered. He was in a room which was dominated by several long tables. On most of them were piles of virgin newspapers which Salmon assumed were this week's *Gazette*. A man was bent over the pile on one of the tables. He had his back to Salmon. He was tall and thin and round-shouldered. Probably the result of bending over interminable newspapers, thought Salmon.

'Go into my office,' said the man, without turning round. 'I'll be with you directly.'

Salmon found the office – it was one of the three doors that led from the main room. The other two were at the back where the hum of the machinery proclaimed that they led to the production side of the newspaper.

Salmon sat in the chair that was obviously reserved for visitors. He noticed that this was the room which had the whitewashed window. It prevented him from seeing out; on the other hand nobody could look inside either.

The man entered. When Salmon saw him face to face he observed that he was older than he had thought. He had a thin face with a straggly moustache and dark hair receding from a high forehead.

'My name is Banbury. What can I do for you?' he demanded as he sat in the main chair behind the desk.

41

'My name is Salmon. I've come to see whether you can give me some information about Roger Stone.'

Banbury gave him a searching stare.

'You're thinking of going to look for him?'

'Yes. Me and my friend. But I've just heard some things about other guys who went to search for him. Apparently they ended up dead.'

'That's right.' Banbury gave Salmon another one of his searching stares.

'So – when was this?'

'When? Let me see. The first body turned up here about six weeks ago. Then the second a couple of weeks later. The third was found last week.'

'What was the connection? How did the sheriff know that they had something to do with Roger Stone?'

'The three of them had all announced that they were going to search for him.'

'I see.'

Banbury subjected Salmon to another one of his stares.

'They also had one other thing in common.'

'What was that?'

'They had all been scalped.'

Salmon's hand automatically flew to his head.

'Yes, you've got a nice head of hair. You'd look good on one of their totem poles.' Banbury roared with laughter.

'Very funny,' snapped Salmon.

'Was there anything else?' demanded Banbury, as he wiped his eyes.

'I don't think so.'

Salmon stood up.

'By the way, do you know that the Indians didn't scalp Custer?'

'Why not?' Salmon paused by the door.

'One theory is that he had a close hair-cut. So his scalp wouldn't look too good on a pole. If I were you, I'd consider going to a barber.' Banbury was again roaring with laughter as Salmon left the building.

CHAPTER 9

In fact Salmon did go to the barber's. Not to have his hair cut but to have a shave. He had several days' growth of beard to get rid of and he never felt comfortable with a beard.

Afterwards he was undecided about his course of action. The evening was drawing in and if he started now for the reservation it would be dark before he arrived there. And riding in the dark was not a very inviting prospect.

He decided to spend the night at a saloon. The one where he had won at arm wrestling was convenient. So he went inside and ordered a room.

When he was shown up to the room, it didn't rate too highly in his estimation. Still, it had that essential piece of furniture – a good bed. When booking the room the saloon keeper had informed him that for an extra fifty cents he could have a warm bath. The idea attracted Salmon. The result was that half an hour after being shown into his room the maid informed him that his bath was ready. She led him down to the back of the saloon where there were several cubicles. She indicated his particular one and handed him a towel. Salmon thanked her and within a few seconds he had sunk into the tub of warm water.

As he relaxed in the water, his thoughts turned to McGee. How was he getting on in bed with Emma? He had known McGee for several years. They had been partners in the circus for four years. During that time McGee had been tempted to stray from the straight and narrow marital path on more than one occasion. Once or twice Salmon had been on hand to prevent it, but he had no doubt that there had been other occasions when he had not been present. And furthermore, he had no doubt that during those periods McGee had conveniently forgotten his church vows to be true to Letitia until death did them part. No, with McGee spending a few nights in bed with Emma, the portents were not in favour of his friend remembering his status as a husband.

Ah, well, fortunately he had no problems in that direction He was faithful to his beloved Jill, and always would be. Even on the occasion when he had spent several nights up a mountain with the beautiful Indian woman, Tandolee, while they were trying to win a bet that rain would come to their town, had not made him deviate from the path of true love. Although on several occasions he had been sorely tempted. There had been the time, for instance, when Tandolee had stood by the pool on the mountain. She had been completely naked. She had stood there for several minutes without saying a word. But the invitation had been as plain as if it had been written in the sky. *Take your clothes off and come into the pool with me.* Even then he had resisted the temptation.

An hour or so later, a refreshed Salmon went down to the bar. It was quite full and he had to wait some time before it was his turn to be served. During that time he listened idly to the saloon singer who was standing on a rostrum and singing 'Shenandoah'.

She had quite a pleasing voice. Her figure, too, was quite attractive. Salmon watched her move to the tune in the current fashion of singers. When she had finished she received a generous round of applause.

Salmon was at last being served by the barman when he realized that she had come over to stand by him.

'Would you like to buy a lady a drink?' she demanded.

It was an unwritten law that if the singer asked you to buy her a drink, you never refused.

'And one for the lady,' added Salmon, as he received his drink.

When she had accepted her whiskey she raised her glass to Salmon.

'Your good health,' she said, with a smile.

Salmon glanced down at her. She was probably in her late twenties. She had a pleasant round face, blonde hair and attractive blue eyes. She was the sort of person Salmon would have expected to be married with at least a couple of children at home in the house.

'You're the guy who beat Drake at arm wrestling earlier this day, aren't you?'

'That's right.'

'I heard about it. May I say congratulations?'

'Thanks.' She really was a pretty woman. The only drawback was that she seemed to be wearing an excessive amount of perfume.

'He's been making my life a misery lately. The trouble with him is that he thinks he's the cock of the walk. Now that you've beaten him maybe it will bring him down a peg or two. By the way, my name's Clara.'

'My name's Salmon. I'm glad that I've helped in some way.'

'Are you stopping to hear the second part of my act?'

47

'I don't see why not. I'm staying in the saloon.'

Her eyes sparkled. 'I'll tell you what I'll do. I'll sing a song just for you.'

'I'm not sure . . .' Salmon began.

'It's a way of saying thank you for beating Drake at arm wrestling. What is your favourite song?'

Salmon thought for a few moments. Then he said: 'I don't suppose you get much call for it up here. But I like 'Dixie'.

'Don't you believe that there isn't much call for it. Most of the guys here know the chorus. Right, 'Dixie' it is.' She stood on tiptoe and kissed him on the cheek. 'And thanks again.'

Salmon watched her leave and prepare to take her place on the rostrum. She whispered something to the pianist before he began to play.

She didn't start with 'Dixie'. Instead she started with another old favourite. 'The Yellow Rose of Texas.' Salmon glanced around. There were several men who were wiping the tears from their eyes as she sang the song. It didn't take a genius to work out that they had come from Texas. Probably in search of the gold which had brought men flocking to the area in the past.

She followed it with an apt song for the gold-seekers – 'Clementine.' The roar of applause she received at the end again testified to how many of the audience had connections with the gold-seekers. By now Salmon was on his second drink.

48

Normally he confined his drinking to a single beer. Even when he was with McGee he wouldn't try to keep up with his companion, who could drink for a couple of hours, imbibing at least eight pints of beer in the process.

Salmon realized that Clara was about to sing 'Dixie' when the pianist struck the first few chords.

Clara came to the front of the rostrum.

'My next song is a request. It's for a guy named Salmon, who some of you may know beat the cowboy, Drake, at arm wrestling here his earlier today.'

Any embarrassment that Salmon would have felt at suddenly being the centre of attraction was alleviated by the loud cheer that greeted the remark. It was obvious that Drake didn't rate very highly in the popularity stakes in the saloon.

'Just for you. Just for you,' said Clara, as she started to sing.

I wish I was in the land of cotton;
Old times there are not forgotten.

When she had finished she received an even bigger round of applause than on the previous occasion. Salmon was no less enthusiastic than the others.

She came over to him.

'That was great.'

'Thanks.'

Before he could stop her she had ordered two whiskeys. He was thinking of refusing one, but she was obviously pleased with his praise. And anyhow, to refuse one would seem churlish.

'You're not from these parts. Where are you from, Salmon?'

'New York. I use to work for a circus.'

The enthusiasm with which she greeted his remark wasn't feigned.

'Tell me about it.'

Salmon began to regale her with some of the lighter sides of circus life. It made Clara laugh on several occasions. She had a pleasant tinkling laugh that Salmon found attractive. The result was that he racked his brains to find more amusing incidents in order to hear her laughter.

He knew that during his recounting of the incidents he had drunk two or three more whiskeys. The barman had insisted on supplying them free of charge. Salmon assumed that since Clara was one of the staff she would have free drinks and therefore her companion would be entitled to the same treatment.

About half an hour later that he realized he was getting drunk. Well, there was only one thing for it. Up the wooden hill, as his grandmother used to say.

'I'm afraid it's past my bedtime,' he told Clara.

'I've got to make an early start in the morning.'

Why did he pronounce start as sthart? It wasn't usually pronounced that way, was it?

The barman had brought two more whiskeys over. A sober Salmon would have observed that he had put a measure of white powder in the drink that he handed to him.

'One for the road,' said Clara, emptying her glass and inviting Salmon to do the same.

Well, what the hell? He had had a very enjoyable evening. What was one more drink? If it meant that he didn't start out for the reservation as early as he had expected, it didn't make any difference. It just meant that he would arrive there later. Clara was watching him with those attractive large blue eyes. If he hadn't been married to Jill, he might even have considered going to bed with Clara. She had a nice figure. Not too skinny, as many of the young women were these days. Her figure Kul was nicely rounded. Especially in the parts that counted.

He realized that she was still waiting for him to finish his drink. He wasn't really a whiskey drinker. He didn't particularly like its taste. That was why he tended to drink it in one swallow.

Too late he realized that there was something wrong with this whiskey. It didn't taste as it should have. It had a bitter taste. Well, there was nothing he could do about it. The sensible thing was just to lie down and go to sleep. The two men whom the barman had stationed behind him caught him as he fell.

CHAPTER 10

The following morning in an upstairs room not far from the newspaper office which Salmon had visited the day before six men had gathered. Although they were discussing Salmon the only one he would have recognized was the barman at the Golden Lode Saloon.

His name was Filton and he was holding forth while the others were hanging on to his words.

'As you know we've got rid of three outsiders who were causing waves. This guy Salmon could be our next threat. He's already said he's going up into the Black Hills. We can't take any chances. There's too much at stake. The only answer is to make sure that he never gets there.'

'You mean that's another job for me?' The question came from the only Indian in the room. He had lived among the white folk for so long that his name had been forgotten. To everyone he was known as Lenny.

The man who was seated at the head of the table, whose name was Calhoun, replied: 'It looks like it. You and Grimshaw, of course.'

While Calhoun was dressed in a tailored dark suit, Grimshaw was casually dressed in a red shirt and jeans.

The only other member of the group to be wearing a suit was a white-haired man named Bilson. Not only was he obviously older than the others, but he gave the appearance of being a wealthy man, with his several gold rings and gold watch chain.

'We've got to make sure that there are no slip-ups. I've invested a few thousand dollars in this enterprise and the last thing I want to see is a slip-up.'

'There won't be, Mr Bilson,' Grimshaw assured him. 'There haven't been any complaints about our other three jobs, have there?'

'No, they seem to be satisfactory.'

'There is one thing though,' put in Filton. 'The other three bodies were discovered in the town.'

'That's right,' said Grimshaw. 'We had to follow each of them for a while. When we caught up with them the end was easy.'

'I think it's putting too much emphasis on the town. What do you think, Deputy?'

The sixth member of the group, who had been

silent until now, was wearing a deputy sheriff's badge. He was in his early thirties and was by far the ugliest of the group. In fact anyone would have to go a long way to find somebody uglier. His name was Goole. He had small piggy eyes set in deep sockets topped by thick black eyebrows. These were capped by straggly hair set above a low fore-head. His nose was long and twisted where it had been broken when he was young and never set properly. His mouth was a thin line which was often set in a bitter expression as he seethed inwardly against the iniquities of a life that had bestowed such a face on him. He had large ears which had presented his boyhood tormentors with a ready-made focus for mockery.

'Yes, I agree,' he stated. 'Three killings in six weeks is putting too much emphasis on the town. It would be better if the next one were outside the town.' He spoke about the prospect of another killing as casually as if he were talking about putting down a dog that had grown too old to continue savouring life.

'This guy, Salmon, will be going back to the Indian reservation soon,' said Filton. 'There must be several places along the way where you can ambush him.'

'I know the best place,' said Lenny. 'It's about five miles outside the town. It's a canyon called Stanton's Canyon.'

'Right,' said Filton. 'You two come back to the saloon. When he's about to move, I'll let you know. It'll take him at least ten minutes to reach the livery stable and fetch his horse. It will give you two plenty of time to get to Stanton's Canyon.'

'Make sure there are no slip-ups,' warned Bilson.

'There won't be,' promised Grimshaw.

CHAPTER 11

Salmon opened his eyes. He was lying in a bed – which was a good thing. His head seemed fairly clear – which was also a good thing. The problem was that there was a female form lying next to him – which wasn't so good.

'You're awake,' said the female.

She was a blonde with large blue eyes – where had he seen her before?

Another thing struck him. He was naked. So was she.

'You remember everything, don't you?'

'No-o.'

'That's a shame.'

'Is it?'

'Yes. Because we made love again and again. I've never had such a night of passionate love.'

Salmon groaned. 'Oh, no!'

'It's nothing to be ashamed of. Most men would

give their right arm to be able to make love as often as you did last night.'

He groaned again. 'Why can't I remember?'

'Well, you'd had too much to drink. Maybe that's the reason.' She moved suggestively against him. 'I'm ready for a repeat performance.'

'Oh, no!' He leapt out of bed. Suddenly realizing his nakedness he tried to cover himself with his hands.

She chuckled. 'There no need to be embarrassed. You've got nothing to hide that I haven't seen a lot of already.'

Some of the events of the evening were coming back to him. 'Why aren't I in my own bed?'

'If you remember, when we were coming up the stairs, I asked: your room or mine? Your answer was your room'. So here you are.'

'Where are my clothes?'

Clara pointed to a bundle in the corner. 'Are you sure you won't come back to bed?'

'Quite sure,' said Salmon, dressing quickly.

'You soon go off a girl, don't you?' she said, sharply.

'I'm sorry. It's nothing personal. It's just that I don't remember anything about last night. If I owe you any money . . .' He took out a few dollars and placed them on the bedside chair.

She jumped out of bed. Seeing her standing naked Salmon would have been the first to admit that she had a very good figure. A very good figure indeed. However, his admiration was short-lived.

'Damn you!' she hissed. 'And damn all men! That's all you think about is money! Money!' She flung the dollar bills on to the floor.

'I'm sorry,' said Salmon, with massive inadequacy, as he picked up the bills.

'Go on. Get out,' she said, in more normal tones.

Salmon did so. Luckily he could remember the number of his room and found it down the corridor. He went in and flopped down on the bed.

Why couldn't he remember the night of passion that Clara alluded to? It was all a blank in his mind. He could remember listening to her singing. He could remember her singing 'Dixie' for him. After that there was very little that he could remember. True, he remembered having a drink or two too many. He had had several whiskeys, which was anathema to him, since he didn't usually drink whiskey. Yes, it must have been the whiskeys. As Clara had said it would all come back to him.

He began to wash with the water in the washbasin. It would be nice, though, to remember some of the passionate events. Wait a minute! That would mean being disloyal to Jill. And he had never been disloyal to her in his life. He had never cheated on her, like other men. Like McGee, for instance.

59

What if he told McGee about last night? And about what Clara had said about their love-making? She was obviously a lady of some considerable experience in these matters. What had she said? *Most men would have given their right aim to have made love the number of times you did last night.* It was nice to know that he had been a lion of love in bed. Even though he couldn't remember anything about it.

On second thoughts, maybe it wasn't something to boast about to McGee. It wasn't the sort of thing to be made public. You never knew – maybe McGee would accidentally let slip the information at some future time. And Jill would get to hear of it. And he knew with one hundred per cent certainty that she would never let him in her bed again.

It was late when he set out for the reservation.

CHAPTER 12

The fact that Salmon was in a hurry probably saved his life. When he came to Stanton's Canyon he rode hell for leather through it. The first indication he had that the day was going to be an eventful one happened when two shots winged their way towards him, only missing him by a few inches.

Salmon's reaction was instantaneous. He slid from the saddle so that he was out of sight of the gunmen on the right hand side of the canyon who were firing at him.

'He's riding like an Indian,' said Lenny, in tones that were a mixture of admiration and disappointment, since he was now unable to get another shot at him.

Who were the gunmen? He knew from the fact that he had glimpsed two flashes that there were two of them. Why were they trying to kill him? Well, there was only one way to find out.

The canyon was long and winding and Salmon was soon out of sight of the gunmen. As he rode he weighed up his chances. The gunmen would only be about half a mile behind him if he rode on and tried to reach the reservation before them. The chances were that they would be able to narrow that gap. That meant that they would be able to fire at him with their rifles. Maybe the next time they would be more successful with their shots. In which case it would be 'Goodbye, Salmon'.

No, his best chance would be to climb one of the paths he had spotted as he rode along. Then, take up a position above the trail. When they came round the bend he would be able to pick off one of them. That should shorten the odds against his joining the heavenly hosts.

He searched impatiently for a suitable path. Its main requirement had to be that it would be wide enough to take his horse. He passed several paths that were probably goat tracks, or maybe used by some other animals, but they were too narrow for his horse. He knew he must be nearing the end of the canyon. When he came to it, of course, all his plan would have to be scrapped, and he would have to take his chance in outriding them.

Just when he was giving up the idea of finding a suitable path, he came across one. It was wide enough for him to ride up it. And it didn't seem too steep for his horse to manage. He swung off the floor and they began their climb.

Every fibre of his being was concentrating on reaching the solitary tree which stood ahead. It was a stunted tree; the sort of tree that you would expect to see growing on a mountainside. But it could mean the difference between safety and being exposed to a hail of bullets from his pursuers.

The path wasn't as easy to negotiate as he had first assumed. He was only halfway to the tree when his horse slipped. For one heart-stopping moment he thought the horse was going to go down on his knees. But thankfully he managed to regain his feet.

'Come on, boy,' said Salmon, encouragingly. 'It's not far now.'

It was true that the tree was now only a hundred yards ahead. But every yard seemed like a nail in his coffin as he knew that his pursuers must be gaining on him. They would come round the bend below as he had done. And they couldn't fail to see a rider struggling up the slope to their right.

Salmon had been in several tricky situations in his lifetime. But in these there had always been McGee present. They looked out for each other. They shared their dangers. So far they had come through relatively unscathed. But here he was on his own.

The sweat was pouring off him even though it

was cool in the canyon. He wasn't wearing a hat and the sweat was running down his forehead. He couldn't take time to brush it aside. Every sinew was being strained to propel his horse forward. He almost carried the horse the last few yards.

But he had made it!

He gasped with relief as he rapidly tied the horse to the tree. He drew out his Winchester from its holster. There was no sign of his pursuers. He lay down on a low ridge which breasted the hillside in front of the tree. It presented him with an ideal place to rest his rifle.

He was aiming at the bend round which the riders would soon appear. Every second that passed was a bonus since it helped him to slow down his breathing, which had been racing after the exertions of the climb He wished he had time to wipe his hand, which was sticky with sweat. But he knew that he couldn't take his eyes off the trail below for a second, even to wipe his hands.

Suddenly there they were. They were accompanied by a small cloud of dust which was kicked up by their horses. It wasn't enough to put Salmon off his aim.

The *crack* of the first bullet sounded unnaturally loud in the confines of the canyon. It hit the first rider in the chest and he toppled awkwardly from his horse. The second rider then made a fatal error. He reined in his horse. It presented Salmon with a perfect target which he eagerly accepted. A bullet sounded again in the canyon. Salmon was surprised to see that his target was an Indian, before he too fell from his horse.

CHAPTER 13

The inhabitants of Caraton were used to seeing dead men. They prided themselves on being blasé about the odd killing. True, there were fewer dead bodies around now than there had been about ten years ago, when Custer's effort for eternal glory had ended in catastrophe. But the Indians had paid the price. They had been rounded up and herded into reservations. True, also, there had been some unexplained killings recently, where dead bodies had mysteriously appeared having first been scalped. But the sight that stirred the inhabitants to register surprise on a particular afternoon was the apparition of a rather large man riding into town, with not one but two corpses slung across the saddle in front of him.

Salmon rode slowly down Main Street. He was aware that he was attracting considerable attention, but he ignored the watchers. Many of them had stopped their perambulation on the sidewalk and were staring, open-mouthed at Salmon's progress. An hour or so ago, having killed his two attackers, he had tried to ascertain who they were. He had examined their corpses for any documents or information about them. The Indian had not carried any identifying papers. In fact he hadn't carried anything. Not even the makings of a cigarette. The other guy, however, provided a clue to his name. It was in the form of an envelope he had obviously received. Fortunately the envelope was in a pouch that was attached to his belt and therefore it wasn't covered with blood as it would have been if he had carried it in his breast pocket.

The envelope was addressed to a Mr Grimshaw, 31, Bargates, Herford. Unfortunately the letter wasn't inside. However, it raised some pleasant memories which Salmon savoured while he was riding back to Caraton. He and McGee had been to Herford. It would have been about a year or so ago. While they were there they had helped to catch some outlaws. Yes, it had been a pleasant episode. Except for one thing. McGee had become involved with a young lady. She was the daughter of the local whiskey-maker. What was her name? Yes, Daisy, that was it. Dan was her father who made very strong whiskey. It must have been something like Dan's whiskey that he had been drinking last night. He still couldn't remember any of the details of his passionate love-making with Clara.

Salmon arrived at the sheriff's office. He dismounted, tied his horse to a hitching rail and grabbed the Indian under one arm. He took hold of Grimshaw under the other arm. He strode towards the office.

There were a couple of boys playing outside the sheriff's office. They stopped their game and stared at the approaching Salmon.

'Would you open the door for me?' he demanded.

One of the boys obeyed with alacrity. Salmon strode into the office with a corpse under each arm. There was only person in the office – the deputy, Goole. He looked up from some papers he had been studying. The sight that met his eyes almost made him fall off his chair with astonishment.

'Wha – Wha – t have you got there?' He managed eventually to articulate the sentence.

'These two guys tried to bushwhack me,' said Salmon. 'I managed to shoot them. I don't know the name of the Indian, But the other guy is named Grimshaw.'

Goole didn't need to be reminded of the name since he had already recognized the two of them. He was slowly recovering his composure.

'Where did this happen?'

'A few miles outside town. In some canyon or other.'

It was almost inconceivable. The two experienced killers had been sent out to shoot the guy in front of him and he had killed, not one, but both of them.

After the initial shock Goole was beginning to think quickly.

'I'll want a signed statement of what exactly happened,' he said.

He showed Salmon into a small room where there was only a chair and a small table. He gave him a pen and some sheets of paper.

'I suppose you can write?' he asked.

Salmon didn't bother to reply.

Back in his office Goole knew he had to decide what to do next. It was obvious that he would have to call another meeting of the committee this evening. Then break the news to them that two of their members were dead. Shot by the guy named Salmon who was now penning his description of the events that had led up to Lenny and Grimshaw being killed.

The only thing in their favour at the moment was that the sheriff was away. He had gone to a funeral in Chicago and wouldn't be back for a few days. So that should give them time to decide what to do with the guy in the other room.

About a quarter of an hour later Salmon appeared. He handed the sheet of paper to Goole. He waved Salmon to a chair while he read it.

He was surprised at the accurate description of the events. To kill the two with two shots must have been some feat of shooting.

'You must be an expert marksman,' observed the deputy.

'I was a sharpshooter in a circus,' replied Salmon.

'That was how you managed to slip off the saddle and ride the horse by clinging to the side?'

'Yes, me and my partner used to do it as part of our act.'

While Salmon had been writing out his report, Goole had been giving the problem about what to do with Salmon a great deal of thought. He had eventually come up with what could be a solution. He put his plan into action.

'I'm afraid I can't deal with this matter myself,' he said. 'I'm only the deputy sheriff. The sheriff is away but we're expecting him back this afternoon. I've got a suggestion to make.'

'Carry on,' said Salmon.

'I suggest you stay here for a couple of hours. You can stay in one of the cells. The door will be open so that you won't be locked in. But you'll be on hand when the sheriff returns.'

'You say he should be here in a couple of hours?'

'That's right. Once he's read your statement you'll be free to go.'

'All right. To be honest I feel a bit tired. I suppose I can always go to sleep in the cell?'

'There's nothing stopping you. None of the other cells is occupied, so nobody will disturb you.'

The deputy led the way to the cells. There were five in all and he led Salmon to the furthest one.

'Here we are. You can make yourself comfortable. The door will be open if you want to come and see me at any time.'

Salmon stretched out on the bed. He watched the deputy leave. Yes, the idea of a couple of hours' sleep was very appealing. Maybe the fact that he hadn't had much sleep last night was now having its effect. It was a pity, though, that he still couldn't remember anything about the passionate lovemaking that Clara had mentioned.

He closed his eyes and in a few seconds was asleep.

When Salmon awoke the first thing he noticed was that it was dark outside the barred window. The window itself was none too clean, having gathered dust over the years and nobody had made any effort to clean it off. He checked his watch. He had been asleep for five hours. The deputy had said that the sheriff should have arrived back three hours ago. Well, he'd better go and sort it out. He didn't intend hanging around here indefinitely.

It was than that he made his second unwelcome discovery. The cell door was locked. When he had come into the cell it had been left open. Now it was locked. Not only that but his gunbelt, which he had hung from the bars, was now missing.

Panic began to set in. What was going on? Why was he now being kept prisoner? He had to find an answer as quickly as he could.

He banged on the door and at the same time shouted at the top of his voice. He kept up the commotion for several minutes. It had no effect, other than giving him a sore hand. The inescapable fact which had began to dawn on him, now became a reality. He was a prisoner in jail in Caraton.

CHAPTER 14

'Why am I being kept here?'

The following morning Salmon addressed the remark to Goole who had appeared in the corridor outside his cell.

'We're checking your story,' replied Goole. 'Your breakfast will be here shortly. In the meantime another of our deputies will be riding out to Stanton's Canyon to verify your story.'

'How can he verify my story? He wasn't there,' said Salmon, irritably.

'He can visit the spot where you claim you shot the two who attacked you.'

'I don't see the point in it.'

'The point is that what you have described in your statement is such a remarkable piece of shooting that there is an element of doubt about it.'

Salmon sighed. 'I've described exactly how it

happened. And where it happened.'

'Yes, the other deputy should be able to find it easily. In the meantime enjoy your breakfast. If everything checks out you should be free later this morning.'

So he had to cool his heels in the cell for another couple of hours. Well, there was nothing he could do about it. The other deputy would find the tree where he had tied his horse. He should find the two spent cartridges to verify his story. That would be that. He would soon be on his way back to the reservation.

He wondered how McGee was progressing. Was his shoulder healing? More important, was he still sleeping with Emma? He thought of his own night of passion with Clara. The night the details of which still eluded him. It would have been nice to have remembered some of them. Even though it would have meant he was being unfaithful to Jill.

It wasn't a couple of hours later that Goole returned. In fact it was nearer four hours. To say that Salmon was getting irritated by having to wait would be a huge understatement. He was livid.

When Goole eventually came down the corridor, Salmon started shouting.

'What the hell do you mean by keeping me here all this time?'

'Take it easy. I've been checking your story and it doesn't quite add up.'

'What do you mean?' demanded Salmon, belligerently.

'You say the two guys shot at you. They missed. You managed to ride further down the canyon and then climb up to a vantage point where you waited until they appeared. Then you shot them.'

'What's wrong with that?'

'The other deputy tried out the manoeuvre with a couple of assistants. He tried it several times. There was no way he could climb to the tree before the gunmen came round the bend and spotted him.'

'My horse is a circus horse. It was specially trained,' said Salmon, impatiently.

'Of course, there is another explanation.'

'What's that?' demanded Salmon, warily.

'That you were waiting for the person whom we've identified as Grimshaw. In fact, that the two of you – you and the Indian – were waiting for him. That you shot him. Then to get rid of the evidence you also shot the Indian.'

'Are you mad?' protested Salmon. 'Why should I kill two people I don't even know?'

'Ah, but maybe you did know them. Maybe you and the Indian have been responsible for the three killings that have taken place in the town in the last couple of weeks.'

'Don't be stupid. I've only just arrived in town. Before that me and my partner only arrived in the

Indian reservation a few days ago. How could I have killed these guys if I wasn't here.'

'Oh, I don't think you killed them personally. I think the Indian killed them and scalped them. But you were the brains behind it.'

'You're not only ugly, but you're stupid as well.' As soon as he had uttered the words and seen the effect they had on Goole, Salmon knew he would regret the remark. Goole's face changed from pink to red to a beetroot colour all in a few seconds.

'I'm not going to stay here arguing with you,' snarled Goole. 'You can stay here while I carry out further investigations.' So saying he stormed off, leaving Salmon to face the prospect of another day lingering in the cell.

CHAPTER 15

Apart from the helper who brought his food Salmon didn't have any visitors until the following morning. He banged on the door from time to time, partly in frustration and partly to attract attention in order to have a further discussion about his plight. But nobody came.

Then, the following morning, he heard the by now familiar sounds of footsteps along the corridor. This time there were two sets of footsteps. He was surprised when he discovered that one set belonged to Clara.

'She's come to see you,' said the helper. 'I'll give you ten minutes.'

After he had gone Salmon said awkwardly. 'It's nice to see you.'

'Are you all right?' she demanded.

'As nice as I'll ever be, locked up in prison.' He managed a smile.

It brought no response from her. Her serious expression did not change.

'When I get out of here, I'll come over to the saloon and buy you a drink,' he promised.

'You're not getting out of here.'

'I think you've got it wrong. You don't understand. The deputy is checking my story again. When he finds that I am telling the truth, he'll let me out.'

'You're the one who don't understand.' There was a new note of urgency in her whispering. 'You're not going to come out alive.'

Salmon experienced a chilly feeling in the pit of his stomach. The kind of feeling that came on when he was in extreme danger. Even though the daylight in the corridor was weak, it was strong enough for him to see the anxiety stamped on Clara's face.

'How much do you know about it?'

'There was a meeting in the saloon. Filton was there and a white-haired man I haven't seen before. And the deputy. I passed the room where they were holding the meeting. Somebody had left the door ajar. So I listened to what they said.'

She checked to see that there was no sign of the helper returning.

'Go on,' said Salmon, impatiently.

'They said they were going to pin the three murders that had been committed in the town on

78

you. They were going to get a group of men together . . .' She paused; the revelations were obviously distressing her.

'Go on.'

'They are going to hang you tomorrow.'

'Oh, no!'

As soon as he gave vent to the cry Salmon wondered whether his tone had been too loud. Would it bring the helper back?

Fortunately everything stayed quiet.

'Where is the sheriff?' demanded Salmon, suddenly aware of how dry his throat had become.

'He's away in Chicago. He won't be back for a few days. That's why the deputy can do what he likes.'

'Is there anybody in town who can help me?' There was desperation in Salmon's voice.

'I can't think of anybody.' There was a sob in her voice that sent Salmon's hopes plummeting down even further.

'Listen, you can ride, can't you,' he said.

'Of course I can.'

'My only hope is if you will ride out to the Indian reservation. See my partner. His name is McGee. Tell him what you've told me.'

'I suppose I could get out there before it gets dark,' she stated, doubtfully.

'The evangelists will look after you once you get there.'

'There's one problem. I haven't got a horse.'

'Take my horse. It's in the livery stable. It's a white horse. Its name is Snowy. If you call him he'll neigh. I trained him to do it in the circus.'

She came to a decision. 'All right. I'll do it.'

There was an awkward pause. It was broken by the sound of the helper returning.

'Good luck,' whispered Salmon, as she turned away.

He knew he would need all the luck that was available and some extra if he was going to get out of this situation.

CHAPTER 16

Perhaps Clara had made a mistake. Yes, that was the most likely explanation. She had been eavesdropping, and she could easily have made a mistake. It would only have required her to get one sentence wrong – maybe she hadn't heard it correctly. And the whole assumption was up the creek.

Maybe somebody had said: *We'll see about trying him in the morning.* Not, as Clara thought she had heard: *We'll see about hanging him in the morning.* It only required one word to be changed and the whole picture changed.

It was good of her to have come over to warn him, though. Even considering she had made a mistake. No doubt she felt that there was still a close bond between them after their passionate love-making of a few nights' ago. Maybe she still regarded him as a prospective lover. Well, he'd

81

have to disappoint her. Any future repeats of their night together was out of the question. He was still a one-woman man. The woman being Jill.

Just suppose for a moment – even though it was a stupid assumption – that Clara had overheard the conversation correctly. She had said that three men were involved in the meeting in the saloon; the saloon keeper himself, the deputy sheriff and another man whom Clara couldn't identify. Just assume also – for the sake of argument – that they were thinking about hanging him in the morning. How did they think they would get away with such a crime? Because it certainly would be a crime of enormous proportions. Even in the West they no longer hanged people without a fair trial. Or at least some sort of trial.

True, the West had been pretty lawless just a few years ago. But things had changed so quickly in the last few years. There were no longer any Indian wars, for example. Of course the main difference was that the railways had come. Well, not exactly as far as Caraton, but to many towns in the West. Law and order had been established. Well, at least to most towns. Why did he think that Caraton was an exception to this civilized process? The obvious answer was that there had been three unexplained killings in the past couple of weeks. *And now the deputy sheriff thought that he had an explanation.*

Salmon shivered even though it was warm in the

82

cell. Why didn't he face facts? He only had to remember the stark worry on Clara's face to know that she had overheard correctly. She wouldn't have come over to warn him if she hadn't. There was only one thing between himself and the prospect of meeting his maker tomorrow morning. Or rather one person. McGee. The last time he had seen him he had been lying in bed with his arm heavily bandaged. Which meant that the odds against Joshua Salmon living to a ripe old age were about the same as him becoming President of the United States.

He thought about writing a farewell letter to Jill. What could he say? That he loved her? She knew that already. And anyhow, if he wrote a farewell letter it would warn the deputy that he already knew about their plan to hang him tomorrow.

Confirmation that Clara had heard correctly about the hanging came later in the evening. The helper who had always prepared his meals, which had consisted of the basic bread and beans, came to see him. 'I'm preparing a special meal for you,' he announced. 'How do you like your steak?'

Who was it who had said: The condemned man ate a hearty meal?

CHAPTER 17

Surprisingly Salmon slept quite well that night. He awoke in the morning and it took him a few seconds to realize that it might be the last time he would wake up.

The realization hit him like a sledge-hammer. Why was God playing such a dirty trick on him? True, he hadn't been to church as often as he should have lately. But on occasional Sundays their wives would drag him and McGee to church. In the past he had attended church regularly – he had even been a choirboy. So why was God deserting him now?

He went to the door. He was about to vent his frustration by banging on it, when he had second thoughts. His only chance of survival lay with McGee. If Clara had delivered the message then presumably McGee would start out early this morning to try to reach Caraton before the hanging took place. In which case he had to try to make sure that the dreaded event took place as late as possible. If he had banged on the door he would be telling the deputy that he was awake. And the deputy could make his arrangements soon. No, his only chance of survival was to play for time.

He put his theory into practice when the deputy arrived.

'There has been a meeting of some of the senior members of the town and the unanimous decision is that they are going to hang you.'

'Oh no!' Salmon put his hand to his throat in a dramatic gesture that would have done credit to a Shakespearean actor.

'There's nothing you can do to prevent it.'

'How – how long have I got to live?' Salmon wondered whether the dramatic pause was too long.

'About half an hour. So if you've got any prayers to say, you'd better say them now.'

Half an hour. That wouldn't give McGee enough time to get to Caraton. 'A condemned man is always allowed one last request.'

'All right,' said the deputy, grudgingly. 'What is it?'

'I want a breakfast. Not just some beans. I want a full breakfast with bacon and eggs and bread.'

The deputy looked as though he was going to refuse. Then he changed his mind.

85

'I'll send across to the saloon to get them to cook one for you. It will mean you'll have an extra half hour or so to live. But I don't suppose it will make any difference.'

It could make all the difference, Salmon decided, as he watched the deputy go down the corridor.

The meal eventually arrived. To Salmon's surprise he quite enjoyed eating it. The deputy called back on two occasions to see whether he had finished. But Salmon spun out eating it as long as he could.

At last he could spin it out no longer. The deputy arrived. 'Are you sure you've finished?' he snapped.

'There's one other thing,' said Salmon.

'Don't say you want to make your will?'

Why hadn't he thought of that? Or at least writing a letter to Jill. Well, it was too late now.

'After I've had a meal, I always have a smoke. It's a last request.' Salmon almost succeeded in putting a dramatic sob into his voice.

'Oh, all right,' growled the deputy.

Salmon took a cigar from his jacket. He and McGee had been in some tight spots before. But he had never known anything as final as this. Would this be his last cigar? He almost choked on it as the thought hit him.

He forced himself to think about the happy

times he had spent with Jill. Most of them had been in New York, before they came out West. The four of them had worked in the circus, and they had been the happiest times of his life. Jill and Letitia had been trick riders in the circus, while he and McGee were the sharpshooters. He wiped a tear from his eye as the memories flooded back.

There was the sound of footsteps in the corridor. This time the deputy was accompanied by a stranger. Both had their guns in their hands.

The deputy opened the cell door. Salmon put on his jacket.

'You won't want that where you're going,' said the stranger.

Salmon thought about smashing his fist into his face. He knew it would bring the instant response of a bullet. It would be a quick end for him. Maybe it would be preferable to being hanged.

He rejected the idea. While there was life, there was still hope.

The sheriff indicated for him to walk ahead of them. Salmon led the way down the corridor. He hadn't reached the end when he felt a painful blow on his head. The result was as sudden as the blow.

Salmon blacked out.

CHAPTER 18

'Our father, which art in heaven, hallowed be thy name. Thy kingdom come, thy will be done . . .'

Why was someone reciting the Lord's prayer? He hadn't heard it for some time. Not since he went to church last. He wasn't in church now, was he? Everything seemed dark. It always seemed dark in church, so maybe he was in church after all.

The other strange thing was that his head seemed muzzy. If his head cleared he'd be able to see exactly where he was.

Another strange thing was that the church seemed to be swaying. He never knew a church to sway. Churches were always solid buildings. Everybody knew that. Churches were reliable and dependable. He remembered when he used to go to church with his Aunt Harriet. The service used to go on and on. You could always depend on that.

Another thing you could depend on was the service. There were always the hymns, followed by prayers. Just as someone was reciting now.

'On earth, as it is in heaven. Give us this day our daily bread. And forgive us our trespasses, as we forgive them that trespass against us . . .'

The church still seemed to be moving. It was swaying like a horse. That was the most ridiculous thing he had ever heard of. How could a church sway like a horse? Wait, a minute! Perhaps he was on a horse. Yes, that was it. He was on a horse.

But they didn't allow horses in churches did they? If they did, he'd never heard of it. Maybe he'd better find out what sort of church this was, that let horses inside it.

Salmon opened his eyes. He saw a dozen or so ruffians grouped round him. They were all on horseback – the same as he was. But their hands weren't tied behind their backs. And they didn't have a noose dangling a few inches in front of them.

The person who was wearing a dog collar continued his rendering of the Lord's Prayer. Salmon knew that his last moments on earth had arrived.

'I'm innocent,' he shouted. 'I haven't committed any crime. I killed a couple of guys who attacked me. That's all I've done. I swear it on my mother's grave.'

His cry went unheeded. The watchers didn't change their expressions. Salmon recognized the deputy who was seated on his horse a short distance away from the others as though to try to dissociate himself from the proceedings.

'Tell them that I'm innocent,' shouted Salmon.

The deputy ignored him. He nodded to the rider who was nearest to Salmon. The rider slipped the noose over Salmon's head.

What a way to die! For a crime he hadn't committed. In a lonely spot outside a godforsaken town far from his beloved family.

He felt the noose tighten round his neck. There was one thing he was determined to do. He would keep a picture of Jill in his mind while he was dying. He would hold her face in his mind until his last breath.

The noose tightened. How long would it take him to die? A few minutes? Of all the ways of dying he had never thought he would be hanged. The noose became unbearably tight.

Next he swung off his horse and was hanging in mid-air. He was choking and there was nothing he could do about it since his hands were tied behind his back. He was aware of the blood pounding in his ears. He tried to suck in deep breaths, but his efforts came to nothing. The noose around his neck was preventing him from breathing. He knew he had reached the end of his life.

Suddenly a strange thing happened. There was the sound of a gunshot. The noose around his neck parted and he was flung on to the ground.

'Take that noose from around his neck,' somebody said. It was a familiar voice. It was McGee.

Somebody obeyed McGee and loosened the noose from around his neck. It was the most marvellous feeling of release he had ever felt in his life.

McGee wasn't alone. There was somebody on his horse. It was Clara. She jumped down and cut the ropes from around his wrists while McGee kept the watchers covered. Salmon jumped up on his horse and Clara jumped up behind him.

McGee tossed a revolver to Salmon and he caught it adroitly. He spoke for the first time.

'It would make me the happiest man in the territory if any of you would go for your guns.'

Nobody moved. Salmon scanned their faces as though he were trying to memorize them.

'Let's go,' said McGee.

Salmon was about to turn his horse round when he caught a movement out of the corner of his eye. It was the deputy and he was going for his gun. Salmon hesitated for a second. In fact it almost appeared that he had left it too late before aiming his own revolver. The deputy had drawn his own gun and was within a hair's breadth of pulling the trigger when Salmon calmly shot him between the eyes.

CHAPTER 19

They were riding like the wind. From time to time they looked behind them. But there was no sign of any pursuers.

When they had ridden a few miles they reined in their horses by a stream and jumped down. Salmon cleared his throat. It was obvious that he was going to make a speech.

'I want to thank both of you for what you did for me. I'll never forget it.' He choked on the last words.

Clara put her arms around him.

'It's McGee you have to thank. For that marvellous shot to snap the rope.'

'There's no need for any thanks,' said McGee, gruffly. 'He'd do the same for me.'

Salmon stared at his partner for a long time.

'Yeah, I suppose so. By the way, what has

happened to your arm? It looks as though it has healed.'

'It has. There's an Indian woman on the reservation. She gave me some home-made ointment to rub on it. It burnt like hell. But it cleared up the wound.'

'I expect Emma helped the cure,' said Salmon, drily.

'Who's Emma?' demanded Clara.

'A friend of McGee's,' replied Salmon.

They set off for the reservation, this time at a more sedate pace. When they arrived there the Children of God greeted Salmon like a long-lost brother.

'I expect you could do with a meal,' Amy fussed.

Salmon didn't admit that he had already had a breakfast. Instead he accepted the offer.

After his meal the Children of God came to their tent singly to congratulate Salmon on his survival. The exceptions to the single visitors were Lizzie and Alice, who came together. They took up the familiar cross-legged Indian position on the floor of the tent.

'What are you going to do next?' demanded Lizzie.

'We came here to try to find Roger Stone. We'll carry on trying to find him,' said McGee.

Salmon didn't receive the statement with any measure of agreement.

'I think we should have second thoughts about it,' he said.

'Oh, I don't mean we should go into the Black Hills tomorrow,' said McGee. 'Have a couple of days to recover. Then we'll go into the mountains.'

'I don't think you're going to have much chance of finding him,' said Alice. 'You could spend a couple of years hunting for him up there, and still not find him.'

'Do you know there are over two hundred caves up there?' said Lizzie. 'He could be holed up in any of them.'

'We came to find Roger Stone and we're not giving up without a try,' said McGee, stubbornly.

Even Clara added her opinion that it was a foolhardy venture.

'He could be anywhere up there,' she said. 'Anything could have happened to him. He could have fallen and frozen to death. Or one of you could fall and not be able to get back here.'

'Thank you for being concerned about our safety,' said McGee. 'Or rather, Salmon's safety,' he added, drily.

Salmon refused to meet his eye. Instead he was examining the roof of the tent as though seeing it for the first time.

'Well, I think it's a foolhardy venture,' announced Clara as she flounced out of the tent.

'We'll have a day's rest. Then we'll start the day

after tomorrow,' said McGee.

Amy was the last to visit their tent. When she heard that they were committed to going up into the Black Hills, she said, simply: 'We'll pray for you.'

CHAPTER 20

The pair of them set off early a couple of days later, as planned. Amy had organized their supplies.

'There should be enough food there for a week,' she said.

Emma came to say her farewell. 'Take care, McGee,' she said. She kissed him on the lips. Salmon tactfully looked the other way.

However, a short while later Clara came to repeat the process; this time with Salmon.

'Look after yourself,' she said, giving him a lingering kiss.

McGee was intrigued by the demonstration of affection.

'What's with you two?' he demanded.

'We're just good friends,' replied Salmon, as he watched Clara disappearing back to her own tent.

The first part of their journey was uneventful. There was a distinct path leading up into the mountains which was easy to follow. They rode for a couple of hours before stopping at a convenient stream. While the horses were drinking the two men munched apples provided by Amy.

'Do you think he's somewhere up there?' demanded Salmon, staring at the snow-covered mountains.

'We'll find out in the next few days,' replied McGee.

When they set off again they soon noticed that the terrain had become steeper. The horses were still able to keep their footing, since McGee's horse, too, had been a circus horse, which meant that he was nimble on his feet.

'I can't see any caves, so far,' said Salmon.

McGee produced a telescope. He swung it around slowly. He too had to admit that he too couldn't spot any caves.

'It's early days yet,' he said.

After another couple of hours' riding the terrain changed. The short grass which they had been riding over gave way to shale. Fortunately the shale was tightly packed and for the moment presented little difficulty to the horses.

An hour later McGee called a halt.

'We'll have our chow and give the horses a rest,' he announced.

They brewed up in the shelter of a large rock. Both scanned the mountain as they ate.

'There must be some wild beasts up here,' suggested Salmon.

'You mean like mountain lions, or bears?'

'Well, it's possible. Just because we haven't seen anything so far doesn't mean that they don't exist.'

'Well, I hope you're wrong.'

'So do I,' said Salmon, with evident feeling.

'I don't mean for us. I mean for Roger Stone.'

'Why?'

'Well if we find him, say he's dead, we'll have to take some evidence back that we have found him.'

'So?'

'If he's been attacked by a mountain lion there might not be much of him left to take back. Especially after the coyotes have finished him off.'

That night they pitched their tent about 1,000 feet further up the trail. Amy had thoughtfully provided them with some wood. They made a fire and were able to brew cups of coffee.

They settled down in their tent.

'If we are disturbed by a mountain lion or a bear, I'll wake you up,' said McGee.

'Shut up and go to sleep,' said Salmon.

The next day their progress was just as uneventful. True, they were nearing the snowline. They could tell, not only by the evidence of their eyes, but also by the fact that everything was getting colder. The wind, too, had increased in strength.

'Roger Stone must have been mad coming up

here to make maps,' said Salmon.

'We're just as mad following him,' said McGee.

'Yes, I suppose you're right.'

Every now and then they would stop so that McGee could scan the landscape with his telescope. But there was no sign of any other living creature, except for the birds that circled around them from time to time.

'What are those birds?' demanded Salmon, when they made one of their stops.

'I don't know. Buzzards maybe. I expect they're waiting to pick your bones.'

'Very funny.'

However, shortly afterwards they saw their first sign of life. It was a stag. The beautiful animal was standing on an outcrop of rock. It seemed to be sniffing the air.

'We're probably downwind of it, and it can't smell us,' whispered McGee, as he reached for his rifle.

'You're not going to shoot him?' demanded a horrified Salmon.

'Of course I am. You never know when he might come in handy.'

McGee killed the stag with one shot.

CHAPTER 21

McGee and Salmon set off early the following morning. The weather was beginning to close in. The colour of the sky had changed to an unhealthy mixture of grey and black. Snowflakes flicked at them at them from time to time as they rode on.

From time to time Salmon thought about suggesting that they should call the whole venture off. How were they expected to try to find somebody in this wilderness when they could now only see a couple of hundred yards in front of them? There was only one reason why he hadn't expressed his opinion that the whole thing was the maddest scheme they had ever embarked upon – and they had tried some hare-brained schemes in their time – the reason was that was that McGee had saved his life a few days ago. As Clara had said, it had been a great shot to part the rope with one bullet from where McGee had been stationed on his horse.

No, he'd go along with the scheme until McGee himself called it off. He brushed the thoughts aside. His whole object now was to concentrate on his riding. They were on a narrow path that skirted the edge of the mountain. It was just wide enough for one horse. One slip and horse and rider could end up a few hundred feet below in the ravine.

His horse snorted as though complaining about the conditions he was forced to endure.

Salmon often talked to his horse. 'It's all right, Snowy,' he explained. 'We can't go on much longer like this. Even McGee will see the sense in turning back soon.'

The snow was now coming down in persistent flakes. Salmon took a tighter grip on the reins. His whole mind was concentrated on the vague figure ahead. McGee was less than fifty yards in front. It was funny the way the snow made him disappear from time to time. When he had been in the circus there had been a conjurer named Lord Anders. While he had been performing his tricks his catch-phrase had been: 'Now you see it. Now you don't.' That was the way it was now with McGee and his horse. It was funny the tricks your mind played when you were in danger.

What danger? They weren't in any danger. True, the snowflakes were getting more persistent. They

102

were swirling around them in silent, white, menacing clouds. Who would have thought that such innocent-looking white, fluffy snowflakes could be so dangerous?

The thought was hammered home to him when Snowy slipped. Or rather he skidded, since he didn't lose his footing completely. He managed to regain his balance with an effort.

'Good horse,' said Salmon His pat on the horse's neck indicated not only a feeling of affection for the animal, but also enormous relief.

How much longer were they going to carry on along this dangerous path? Had he been saved from certain death a couple of days ago, only to meet his end now by falling down the mountainside and freezing to death? He knew with one hundred per cent certainty that if either of them slipped off the path, then that would be the end of their lives. They would soon freeze to death. The weather had grown so cold that even through his thick gloves he could feel that his fingers had become numb. There was no doubt that freezing to death was high on his list as his way of dying.

This was utterly stupid, to carry on in these conditions. The snow was getting more and more persistent. It was swirling round him so that visibility was reduced to a mere few yards. Then from time to time the snow would clear, as though playing some game with him. When it did clear he was able to see McGee clearly. Then in a few seconds he would disappear again.

'We should go back,' he shouted.

The words seemed to hang in the air, as though mocking him. There was no way that McGee could hear him with the way the wind now howling.

The next sound, however, they both heard. It was the sound of a rifle shot.

'Somebody's shooting at us,' shouted McGee.

CHAPTER 22

Strangely the snow cleared and visibility improved considerably. Enough for them to see that they had come to the end of the tortuous and dangerous path. They were now on a fairly large plateau. And facing them was what appeared at first sight to be a bear. He was wearing a bear's skin with a hat made from the same animal. The main difference was his whiskered face. Also there was nothing bearlike about the rifle which he held steadily in his hand.

'Keep going on your way, misters,' said the apparition.

'We weren't thinking of stopping, anyway,' said McGee, who was the first to recover. He shifted slightly in his saddle.

'Don't think of drawing that gun,' said the man with the rifle. 'I can kill the two of you before you draw your guns.'

'Oh, let's go on our way,' said Salmon. 'We don't want to stop here and argue with him.' He had forgotten that ten minutes ago he had been utterly in favour of turning back. Now he was advising McGee to carry on.

'I suppose you're right,' said McGee, regretfully. He spurred his horse to start moving.

'Hold on a minute,' said the stranger. 'Is that Old Groaner?'

McGee reined in his horse. 'Who?'

'Old Groaner. The stag you've got there.' The stranger came close to McGee's horse to examine him. 'Yes, it is. Well I'll be dammed. I've been trying to kill him for the past couple of years. And here you come up here and with a lucky shot you manage to get him.'

'It wasn't a lucky shot,' said McGee, shortly.

'Well, anyhow, you've killed him. What are you going to do with him?'

'I don't know. When we get back to the reservation, we'll give him to the ladies to cook. They say that the steaks are excellent.'

The appearance of Old Groaner had changed the stranger's tone of voice. It now became friendly.

'I'll tell you what I'll do. I'll buy him off you.'

At the thought of receiving some extra money, McGee's interest soared. Whereas a moment ago his only interest had been in riding away from the stranger with the gun, now he turned his attention to the stag. Even caressing it lovingly.

'I wasn't thinking of getting rid of it,' said McGee.

'You can keep the antlers. I haven't any use for them up here.'

'He must be worth at least fifty dollars,' said McGee. Actually he had no idea how much the stag was worth. He just plucked the figure out of the air.

'I haven't any money,' said the stranger.

'Then how do you think you're going to pay for him?' demanded McGee, irritably.

'With gold. I'll give you a nugget each. It'll be worth more than your fifty dollars.'

'You're a prospector,' said Salmon.

'You've got in one, son. I've been a prospector for the past twenty years. Ever since the gold rush in these here hills.'

'So you stayed on?' said McGee.

'That's right. You'd better come into my cave. We'll do the deal there.'

The stranger's cave was on the far side of the plateau.

'By the way, my name's Ben,' he said, as he led them inside.

McGee introduced themselves. He was surprised to find that the cave was fairly large. It was comfortably decorated not only with bearskins on the floors, but also hung from the walls.

'It's very cosy,' said Salmon.

'It's home,' replied Ben. McGee had untied Old Groaner from his saddle. He handed him to Ben who accepted him carefully. 'He'll keep me in steaks for a few months,' he informed them.

'You mentioned something about payment,' prompted McGee.

Ben fetched a small bag from the pocket of a jacket that was hanging on a hook. He emptied a couple of dozen or so gold nuggets on to a low table. He selected two which were about the same size.

'Here.' He gave one each to McGee and Salmon. 'You should be able to get fifty dollars each for them.'

'Thanks,' said Salmon.

McGee added his thanks. 'So you've found a gold seam?' demanded McGee.

'You don't think I'll tell you, do you, son?'

'No,' replied McGee. 'Anyhow, keep it to yourself.'

'That's what I've done for the past twenty-five years,' replied Ben. 'Before you go I can offer you some coffee. I can't give you any chow because I only make one meal in the evening.'

While Ben was brewing the coffee. Salmon went to fetch some apples which Amy had put in their saddlebags. He handed a couple to Ben who accepted them gratefully.

'You know, that's one of the things I miss about living up here. I don't get any fruit.' When he had made the coffee and the two visitors had produced their own cups, Ben said: 'You haven't told me what you're doing in this godforsaken part of the world.'

'We're looking for Roger Stone,' stated McGee.

'Roger Stone? He's the guy who said he'd come here to make maps?'

'That's right,' said McGee.

'Did you see him?' demanded Salmon.

'Yes, I saw him.'

'What do you mean, he said he'd come here to make maps?' demanded McGee.

'Nobody in their right mind would believe that. You've seen what the weather is like outside. And anyway he didn't have any map equipment with him.'

'Didn't he now,' said McGee, thoughtfully.

'No, and I'll tell you another thing. A few days after he came here, two other men came here looking for him. The same as you two are.'

'I wonder if they found him?' said Salmon.

'Oh, yes. They found him all right. He was staying in a cave about a hundred yards away. They were bound to have seen his horse. They couldn't have missed him.'

'So they found him,' said McGee. 'Why was the

109

advertisement in the newspaper asking for somebody else to trace him?'

'Maybe these two guys didn't want to advertise
the fact that they had found him,' stated Salmon.

'You are dead right, they wouldn't,' said Ben,
with such emphasis that the duo stared at him with
surprise.

'Why wouldn't they want to advertise the fact
that they had found him?' persisted Salmon.

'Because they shot him.'

CHAPTER 23

Half an hour later Salmon and McGee were riding back down the trail they had ridden along earlier. The snow had eased and was now only coming in slight flurries. They made no effort to communicate with each other. They were still travelling in single file and any conversation was difficult. Anyhow, they were both trying to come to terms with the scene they had witnessed when they had entered Roger Stone's cave.

Ben had half-prepared them for a shock by revealing that Stone had been shot. But the real horror lay in seeing the pile of bones just inside the entrance to the cave. They stared at the remains of Stone for several moments.

'The coyotes must have finished him off,' said Salmon, eventually.

'Or wolves,' suggested McGee.

There was a long pause while they digested the

implication of their grisly find.

'Well, we found him,' said Salmon, eventually. 'I don't suppose we'll get any payment for that.'

McGee was looking around the cave. 'Ben was right,' he said.

'What do you mean?' demanded Salmon.

'For a man who was supposed to have come here to make maps there is no sign of any paper here.'

Salmon joined in the search. It didn't take him long to confirm McGee's statement. 'Whoever shot him also took away his gun,' he observed.

'There's nothing to say who he was,' said McGee. Then he changed his tone when he bent down closed to the body. 'Hold on, there might be something.' Among the pile of bones he unearthed a ring. He blew the dust away from it. 'Look, it's got his initials on it. R.S.'

Salmon examined the ring with interest. 'At least it might be something to help those in charge of the newspaper believe that we did find him,' he remarked, with growing excitement.

'Yes, this ring could be a valuable piece of evidence,' said McGee, putting it in his wallet.

That night they set up camp in the same spot where they had camped on their way up the mountains. There wasn't much in the way of conversation between them. Both were looking forward to getting back to the reservation.

When they did get back, late the following day,

the Children of God rushed out to meet them.

'You're back safe,' said Amy, with huge relief in her voice.

The others gathered around. 'Did you find him?' demanded Emma.

'Yes. He was dead,' stated Salmon.

'Well, you've got it out of your system,' said Clara. 'Maybe you can get on with living your life.'

'Where did you get that?' demanded Flora, pointing to the antlers that McGee had brought back with him. 'Did you find it?'

'I shot a stag,' stated McGee.

'Oh, no!' exclaimed Emma. 'They're such lovely creatures.'

'Where is it?' demanded Flora.

'We gave it to an old prospector we found up in the mountains,' explained Salmon.

It was obvious that the news that McGee had shot a stag had poured cold water over the enthusiastic reception they would have received. The evangelists filed away slowly back to their own tents. The only one who stayed behind was Clara.

'You've upset their sensibilities,' she informed the two men.

'What about you?' demanded McGee.' It doesn't seem to have bothered you.'

'I was brought up on a farm,' she explained. 'Killing animals was a part of our daily existence. Although I don't see why you killed a stag if you

113

couldn't eat it.'

Salmon explained how they had given the stag to Ben and how it would keep him in steaks for a while.

'I suppose in the end something useful came out of it,' she conceded.

'He gave us this in exchange,' Salmon showed her the gold nugget.

Clara was obviously impressed. 'You should be able to get quite a few dollars for that. It'll help to make your trip up the mountains worthwhile.'

McGee chipped in. 'The other thing we brought back was this.' He showed her the ring they had found among Stone's bones. 'It's got Roger Stone's initials on it,' he explained.

'Don't show it to anybody else,' she said, with a degree of urgency in her voice. 'It could be a dangerous thing to do. Just forget about Roger Stone and go back to your wives. If you try to claim the money about Stone's disappearance you could be in very big trouble. Not even your sharpshooting skills would be able to get you out of it.'

114

CHAPTER 24

The following morning McGee and Salmon set out for Caraton. Salmon knew he had the unpleasant task ahead of him of explaining to the sheriff how he had killed his deputy.

When they entered the sheriff's office they found a weather-beaten middle-aged man seated behind his desk. He looked more like a farmer than a sheriff.

They introduced themselves and after shaking hands, the sheriff said: 'So you're the big guy who shot my deputy.'

'I'm afraid I didn't have any choice,' said Salmon.

'You'd better give me the whole story,' said the sheriff, taking out a packet of cigars and offering them to the pair.

When the cigars were lit, Salmon began his

story. The sheriff listened expressionlessly until he came to the part where the deputy refused to believe his story about shooting his attackers.

'There was no need for him to make an issue of it,' said the sheriff. 'Our jurisdiction only extends for three miles outside the town. That canyon is beyond the limit.'

Salmon continued his story. When he came to hanging it was obvious that the sheriff was boiling over with anger.

'The bastard!' he snapped. 'No one can be hanged without a trial. It's one of the corner-stones of the rule of law.'

'Well they tried to hang me,' said Salmon. 'If it hadn't been for my friend here, they would have succeeded.'

'I hear you parted the rope with one shot.' The sheriff addressed the remark to McGee.

'We used to be sharpshooters in a circus,' explained McGee.

They left the office shortly afterwards, having received the sheriff's assurance that there would be no charges brought against Salmon.

'To tell you the truth I'm glad to have got rid of him,' said the sheriff. 'I never appointed him myself. He was appointed by some of the town councillors.'

'Where do we go now?' demanded Salmon.

'I'm going to the telegraph office to send a

116

telegram saying that we found Roger Stone. Or at least we found what was left of him.'

'I'm going to the *Gazette* office,' said Salmon. 'The guy there said we'd never find him. I'm going to tell him how wrong he was.'

Salmon entered the *Gazette* office and found Banbury studying a news page.

'Sit down,' he said, waving Salmon to a chair. 'I'll be with you in a minute.'

It was nearer five minutes when he eventually gave Salmon his full attention. 'Now,' he said, with a smile. 'How can you brighten my morning?'

'You said that we'd never find Roger Stone,' replied Salmon. 'Well, we found him.'

'That's good news. Or is it?' he asked, seeing the expression on Salmon's face.

'We found him a few thousand feet up the Black Hills. He was dead.'

'So that isn't good news.'

'He'd been eaten by coyotes. Or maybe wolves.'

'OK. You'd better give me the full story.' He drew a pad of paper towards himself and prepared to write down the events as described by Salmon.

At the end of the recital Banbury said with feeling. 'That wasn't a very pleasant way to die. How did you identify him?'

Salmon showed him the gold ring they had found among the bones.

Banbury examined it. 'Yes, that's sufficient

evidence. You may still be entitled to the thousand dollars.'

'We'll see,' replied Salmon. 'My friend is sending a telegram to find out whether we'll get it or not.'

'Is that the guy who saved your life by parting the rope that they were going to hang you with?'

'That's right. His name is McGee.'

'You'd better give me the exact details of the hanging,' said Banbury. 'There've been so many conflicting stories. In one of them McGee shot the deputy after shooting at the rope.'

'That was me. I shot the deputy.'

'You two do seem to go in for a lot of killing.'

Salmon scowled.

Banbury held up his hand in an apologetic gesture. 'All right. It was only a joke,' he announced. 'By the way, you didn't see the resident gold prospector up in the hills?'

'You mean Ben? Yes, he was the one who pointed out where we would find Stone's body.'

'Well, well. So Ben is still alive? The coyotes haven't eaten him yet?'

'He gave me this.' Salmon showed the gold nugget to Banbury.

The reporter examined it. 'I'm not an expert, but I would think it's worth quite a few dollars.'

Shortly afterwards Salmon left.

'If you kill any more people let me know,' said

Banbury, as he roared with laughter at his joke.

Salmon met McGee outside the telegraph office.

'I've sent the telegram to the Pinkerton Agency.'

'The Pinkerton Agency?' said Salmon, with surprise.

'The article in the newspaper only gave an address. It didn't say who to send it to. The telegraph clerk looked it up. He said the Pinkerton Agency, in Chicago.'

'Maybe we'll stand a chance of getting our money,' said Salmon.

'Maybe you'll be glad we came after all,' stated McGee.

CHAPTER 25

Two days' later the Pinkerton office in Chicago received a telegram. The director, Burke, called his subordinate, Grey, into his office. Burke was a heavy-featured man with a large black moustache. His subordinates joked that they could tell what sort of temper he was in by the way his moustache either drooped or held its usual position. When Grey entered he saw that the moustache was definitely drooping.

Burke waved Grey to a chair. 'I've had this telegram from Caraton. Two guys have found Roger Stone, or what's left of him.'

'He's dead?' Grey queried.

Burke nodded. 'These two guys, McGee and Salmon, found his body a few thousand feet up in the Black Hills.'

'What happened to him?'

'It says here,' Burke waved the telegram, 'that he

had been shot by two men. The coyotes finished him off.'

Grey shuddered. 'What a way to die.'

'Yeah. We'll have to see that his widow gets suitable compensation.'

'What about paying these two guys who found the body?'

'They say that they've got evidence it was Stone who was killed. They've got his ring with the initials on it.'

'Yes, Stone always wore that ring.'

'I suppose we'll have to pay those guys. Anyhow it's not the Agency's money. A government department got in touch with us to send an agent to Caraton. So I'll send the thousand dollars to Caraton and the government department can recompense us.'

'Did you say those guys' names are McGee and Salmon?'

Burke studied the telegram. 'That's what it says here.'

'I've heard about them. They are two sharpshooters. I remember reading in the newspaper how they helped to catch a gang of outlaws in Herford.'

'Sharpshooters, eh?' Burke leaned back in his chair which creaked under his weight. 'It says here that they've got descriptions of the two men who killed Stone.'

'We could always offer them extra payment if

they caught these two men.'

'That's not a bad idea,' said Burke. 'We'll offer them a thousand dollars each. The government department can pay.'

'No, definitely not,' said Salmon.

They had collected the telegram from the telegraph office and McGee had read it to Salmon.

'Think of it. Another thousand dollars each if we find Roger Stone's killers.'

'Think of it. Our two corpses lying on slabs in the morgue.'

'You're always looking on the dark side,' said McGee.

'Salmon is right. Caraton is a dangerous town to be in,' said Clara, who had accompanied them to the telegraph office.

'People get hanged for no reason at all,' said Salmon, automatically rubbing his neck.

'The deputy sheriff is dead. The sheriff is back and he accepted your explanation. He even seemed glad to have got rid of him,' persisted McGee.

'There were a dozen or so ruffians who had come to see me hanged. They could be friends of the deputy, waiting to get even with me.'

'I don't think you're right there, Salmon,' said Clara. 'They were just scum that the deputy had picked up in a couple of saloons. He probably paid them a dollar each to come to see you being hanged.'

'Well, anyhow, I don't see why we should stay,' said Salmon, stubbornly. 'We'll go to the bank. We'll collect our money. And first thing tomorrow we'll be on our way home.'

'What about Clara?' demanded McGee, drawing her into the conversation seeing that his own powers of persuasion were failing.

'I always knew that Salmon would leave me at some time in the future,' she said, with downcast eyes.

McGee sighed. He realized that he might as well admit defeat.

'All right,' he said. 'We'll collect the money from the bank. Then we'll have a good meal.'

'Then?' demanded Salmon.

'Tomorrow we'll be on our way home,' he promised.

Collecting their money from the bank wasn't easy. Pinkerton Detective Agency had been in touch with the bank. The manager, who knew Clara, asked her if she could identify them. She said she could. Once their identity was established the manager said they could come back tomorrow for their money.

With their great expectations in mind, McGee said, 'Now we'll have the best steaks in town. Where do you advise us to go, Clara?'

She was considering where would be the best place for their farewell meal when a strange sight came into view. It looked like a very large iron boiler on a wagon. It was being drawn by two horses. Behind it was another wagon. This had been built up in the form of a house. It had a step leading up to the door and a window with curtains.

'Do you see what I see?' demanded McGee.

'I think so,' replied Salmon.

Clara looked from one man to the other. Then back at the two wagons, which had now reached where they were standing.

Suddenly the door of the second wagon was flung open. A pretty young girl in her late teens jumped down. It was Daisy.

'McGee!' she shouted and dashing to the side-walk flung herself into his arms.

McGee kissed her and finally disentangled himself.

'I see you know each other,' said Clara, drily.

'McGee is the most scheming, conniving, lying bastard you could ever meet,' replied Daisy.

'That about sums him up,' said Salmon.

CHAPTER 26

A short while later the four were seated in the strange-looking caravan. Also inside were two men, Dan, who was Daisy's father, and an Indian, Harold. Because there was very little room inside the caravan, Daisy was happily sitting on McGee's knee.

'So what are you two doing in this part of the world?' demanded Dan.

'It's a long story,' said McGee. 'We were just going out to have a meal. You three are invited.'

'I'll have to make myself pretty first,' said Daisy.

'You're pretty enough as you are,' said McGee, automatically. She pushed her tongue out at him.

A quarter of an hour later they were seated in the Golden Nugget hotel. It had been selected by Clara as the place with the best steaks in town.

When they had finished enjoying their steaks, Dan repeated his question.

McGee explained how they had come here to try to find a man named Roger Stone. They had found him but they were too late. He had already been shot and the coyotes had eaten him. Daisy buried her head in McGee's shoulder at the recital of the gruesome events.

'We'll be coming tomorrow to collect the five hundred dollars each that we were awarded for finding him,' continued Salmon. 'We didn't know it but he was a Pinkerton agent. That was why they were eager to find him.'

'So what brings you three to this part of the world,' demanded McGee. 'It's a long way from Herford.'

'Things were pretty dead there . . .' began Dan.

'Especially after you left me in the lurch,' interrupted Daisy.

McGee ignored her. 'So what makes you think you will sell more of your whiskey here?'

'I met this guy named Bilson in Herford. He sampled my whiskey. He was so impressed that he ordered a hundred bottles.'

'The only snag was we had to come to Caraton,' said Daisy. 'But now it's lucky we came, or we wouldn't have met you again.' She nibbled McGee's ear.

'That's a lot of whiskey,' said Salmon.

'How much do you usually sell in, say, a week?' asked Clara.

'I don't know. It varies. Say about a couple of dozen bottles. If there's a special event, like a rodeo for example, I could sell as many as a hundred.'

'And if McGee's around we always sell more,' stated Daisy.

'Did this guy give you any advance payment?' demanded McGee.

'Yes. He gave me hundred dollars.'

'Dad, you said he only gave you fifty,' complained Daisy.

'Can you describe this man?' asked Clara.

'He was a white-haired man. I'd say he was in his fifties.'

'He had a gold watch and he was wearing several gold rings,' said Daisy.

'It's the same man I saw talking to the deputy – the one you killed,' Clara said to Salmon.

'You killed a deputy sheriff?' demanded Dan.

'He was a crooked deputy,' said Salmon.

'A hundred bottles of whiskey can only mean one thing,' said Clara. 'They want it for the army.'

'There's an army post stationed a couple of miles from the Indian reservation,' said McGee.

'There's at least fifty soldiers there. Probably more,' stated Salmon.

'Yes, I suppose that makes sense,' said Dan, thoughtfully.

'They haven't got any facilities,' said McGee.

'They're probably never allowed into town.'

'You're right,' said Clara.

'So whoever is in charge must have decided to brighten up their existence,' McGee concluded.

'I could brighten up yours,' Daisy whispered in his ear.

'So it looks as though we've solved the reason for you coming to Caraton,' said Salmon.

As they left the hotel, Dan said, 'I think this calls for a celebration. How about trying my latest brew?'

'I never thought you'd ask,' said McGee.

'I'm afraid you'll have to excuse me,' said Clara. 'I've got to get back to the saloon to practise my songs.'

'You're a saloon singer?' demanded a surprised Daisy.

'That's right.'

'Can I come and listen to you?' she demanded, eagerly. 'I've always wanted to be a saloon singer.'

Clara smiled at her enthusiasm. 'Why not? As long as your father gives you permission.'

'I don't have to ask his permission. I've gone eighteen. I'm a big girl now, aren't I, McGee?'

McGee chose to ignore the remark as he followed the men into the caravan.

CHAPTER 27

In an upstairs room not far from the newspaper office five men had gathered. Salmon would have recognized the barman of the Golden Lode, Filton. He had been plying him with drinks on the night he had passed out. And finally given him a drink which Salmon was later certain had been drugged.

Salmon wouldn't have recognized the other four. If Clara had seen them she would have recognized the white-haired man as Calhoun, the man she had spotted through the partly open door in the saloon.

If Ben had been there he would have recognized the two men as the ones who killed Roger Stone. He wouldn't have known their names. They were Mallet and Thorpe.

'Look at this!' Calhoun flung the copy of the *Caraton Gazette* on to the table. 'This guy Salmon is boasting about the fact that he killed three of our consortium.'

'What's a consortium, boss?' demanded Thorpe. Neither he nor Mallet were renowned for having any large measure of intelligence.

'It means we're all together in this venture,' said Calhoun, impatiently.

'We've killed three people already,' said Mallet. 'One more won't make any difference.'

'Four,' said Thorpe. 'You're forgetting that guy Stone up in the Black Hills.'

'Oh, yeah,' replied his accomplice.

'It certainly makes sense to get rid of Salmon,' said Filton. 'I spotted him as trouble the first time he walked into my saloon.'

'Isn't he friendly with your singer – what's-her-name?' demanded Bilson, entering the conversation for the first time.

'Too friendly,' snapped Filton. 'I put a sleeping potion in his drink the first time he stayed in the saloon. I thought you two could get rid of him then. But Clara had him put in her bed and so there was no point in me getting in touch with you.'

'I heard she was at the hanging,' persisted Calhoun.

'That's right,' said Thorpe. 'Me and Mallet were there. Your singer came in with the guy who shot the rope.'

'It was a great shot,' said Mallet, appreciatively.

'Never mind about that,' snapped Calhoun. 'This guy has made us look like a bunch of fools. There were three extra people seated around this table the last time we met. This guy Salmon has killed them all.'

'You should have let us go after him in the canyon, boss, instead of Grimshaw and Lenny,' said Mallet.

'Yes, the whole thing was a fiasco,' agreed Calhoun.

'What's a fiasco, boss?' demanded Thorpe.

Calhoun put his hands to his head. 'Why do I have to suffer such idiots as you two?' he wailed.

'Because we're needed,' said Mallet.

'Yes, unfortunately that's true,' replied Calhoun in more placid tones.

'Well I think we should put it to a vote,' stated Bilson. 'Who's in favour of getting rid of Salmon?'

Four hands shot up.

'What about you?' demanded Calhoun.

'Oh, I'm in favour as well,' replied Bilson. 'The only slight problem we might have is that he always seems to be accompanied by somebody.'

'Who – the singer?' demanded Thorpe.

'No, you fool,' said Calhoun. 'The other guy, McGee.'

'The one who shot the rope,' supplied Mallet.

'Yeah, I wouldn't like to meet him in a fair fight,' said Thorpe.

131

'You've never met anybody in a fair fight,' said Mallet. He began to laugh. His laughter broke the ice which had been apparent in their previous conversation. Soon Thorpe began to laugh. The other three soon had smiles on their faces. The laughter became infectious. It went on for several minutes before one by one they stopped laughing.

'So that's settled,' said Calhoun, after a collective pause for everyone to get back to normality.

'What's settled?' demanded Thorpe.

'That we kill the two of them. For the usual fee, of course,' said Mallet.

'For the usual fee,' Calhoun concurred.

CHAPTER 28

When Daisy returned to the caravan a couple of hours later she found that the three people inside were asleep. She banged some dishes noisily in order to wake them up.

'Anybody for coffee?' she asked, cheerfully.

'That's one thing about your whiskey,' said Salmon, through a yawn. 'It tastes good and you can have a sleep after it.'

'Clara's got a soft spot for you. Especially after you two spent the night together,' said Daisy.

This was news to McGee, who looked at his friend with new-found interest.

'I was drugged,' explained an embarrassed Salmon. 'The owner of the saloon was one of the gang who wanted to get rid of me. Clara had me put into her bed because she thought it might be dangerous for me to be in my own bed.'

'Well, well, so you spent the night in bed with

133

Clara,' said McGee, still staring with interest at his friend.

'Nothing happened,' protested Salmon. 'As I said, I was drugged.'

'Someone under the influence of drugs often cannot remember what has happened,' said Harold.

It was the first time he had spoken and the others looked at him with surprise.

'Maybe you're right, Harold,' said Dan. 'But we've got some work to do to get our bottles ready.'

'How many did you say you've got to get ready for Mr Bilson?' demanded McGee.

'One hundred. He didn't say where he wants them. But he said he'll arrange the transport.'

McGee and Salmon left shortly afterwards. Daisy gave McGee a long lingering kiss.

When they arrived at the reservation they were met by Emma. She kissed McGee, then stood back with displeasure written on her face.

'You've been drinking,' she said.

'We met an old friend. He brews whiskey.'

'Strong drink is the abomination of mankind,' she stated piously.

McGee handed her a large bag of boiled sweets which he had bought while in the town. 'Share these out with your friends,' he said.

'And don't think you can bribe me with these,'

she retorted, as she went off to join the other ladies.

'I think I'll have another rest,' said McGee.

'I think that's a good idea,' said Salmon 'It must be Dan's whiskey,' he added.

A couple of hours later they were awakened by the sounds of singing. McGee, who was the first to awake said: 'It's the Children of God.'

They went outside and found the Children of God were singing one of their hymn tunes. Amy was conducting.

When they had finished she said to the two of them. 'Why don't you join us?'

'No thanks,' said McGee. 'We've got a few things to sort out before we leave tomorrow.'

CHAPTER 29

When Salmon and McGee rode into Caraton the next day they found that the money hadn't been transferred to the bank.

'It should definitely be here tomorrow,' said the cashier.

'That's all right. We're in no hurry,' said McGee.

'I am,' said Salmon. 'I want to get back to Jill.'

'After what happened between you and Clara?' said McGee.

'You can talk. What about the nights you spent in bed with Emma?'

'Yes, well, that was to help me to recuperate.'

'That's the funniest description I've ever heard it given.'

McGee went to see Dan and Daisy while Salmon went to the Golden Lode saloon to see Clara.

The saloon was empty and she was sitting on the piano stool, playing a song that Salmon hadn't heard before. She looked up and smiled when she saw who had just entered.

'I didn't know you played the piano,' said Salmon.

'Yes, I used to give piano lessons to young children. But there's no call for it in this town,' she ended on a bitter note.

Salmon stood somewhat embarrassed by the piano. 'I'm not very good at making speeches,' he began.

'Then don't make them.' Her smile took the sting out of her words.

'What I want to say is that I'll be eternally grateful for your help. By making sure I slept in your bed in the first place. And by fetching McGee in time to save my life.'

It was Clara's turn to appear embarrassed. 'It was lucky I was in the right place at the right time,' she said.

'Well anyhow, I want you have this.' Salmon produced the gold nugget he had received from Ben.

She looked at it with astonishment. 'But it could be worth as much as a hundred dollars.'

'I've no idea how much it's worth. The guy who is the last prospector up in the Black Hills gave it to me. He gave one to McGee, too.'

'I can't take it. It's worth too much money,' she said, positively.

'Please take it. If you don't I'll put you over my knee and spank you.'

'That would be nice,' she said, with a smile.

'You will take it, won't you? It might even be enough to help you to get to a large town. Say Chicago.'

'Yes, that would be lovely,' she said, dreamily. She came to a decision. 'All right, I'll take it.'

'Thanks,' said Salmon, simply.

'Why didn't I meet you before Jill did?' she said, half to herself. 'Well, that's the story of my life.'

'What was the song you were paying when I came in?' asked Salmon, anxious to change the subject.

'It's called "Greensleeves".' She played the intro- duction. 'Just for you. Just for you, Salmon,' she said as she began to sing.

For oh, Greensleeves was all my joy;
For oh, Greensleeves was my delight.
For oh, Greensleeves was my heart of gold;
My lovely lady Greensleeves . . .

Salmon left shortly afterwards, having received a lingering farewell kiss from Clara. On his way back to Dan's caravan Salmon changed his mind. Instead he called in at the *Gazette* ofices.

'Well, if it isn't my favourite news reporter,' said Banbury. 'I was just making some coffee,' he added. 'Would you like a cup?'

Salmon accepted the offer.

'What news have you to impart today?'

'No news. Just a question. Why has a guy named Bilson ordered one hundred bottles of whiskey, to be delivered today?'

'That's a good question.' Banbury scratched his chin thoughtfully. 'I assume you're talking about the colourful caravan and the huge still which has blotted our fair town.'

'Some fair town,' said Salmon, scornfully.

'One hundred. That's a lot of whiskey. Of course the immediate answer that comes to mind is that he intends supplying it to the Indians.'

'But that's illegal, isn't it?'

'Everything that goes on in this town is illegal,' said Banbury, dismissively. 'They've even been known to hang people without a trial.'

'I take your point,' said Salmon.

'Let's consider the implications a little further,' said Banbury. 'If we have a hundred or so Indians from the reservation who have each drunk at least a bottle of whiskey it could release all their bottled-up hatred of us white folk – if you'll excuse the pun.'

'You mean they could attack some white folk?' demanded Salmon.

'I mean they could attack the town.'

Salmon was deep in thought as he finished his coffee.

'As our roving reporter,' said Banbury, 'You are in an ideal position to report on any unusual activities in the reservation. You have access to the place which is denied to us ordinary mortals.'

'I could ask the Children of God to watch out for any unusual activity,' said Salmon.

'My guess would be if they intend smuggling a hundred bottles of whiskey into the reservation then this guy Bilson and his friends would do it tonight. When the Children of God are asleep.'

'I suppose you're right,' said Salmon.

'It can only mean one thing,' said Banbury. 'It means that you and your friend McGee must keep watch tonight.'

'To think I was looking forward to a good night's sleep,' said Salmon, ruefully.

CHAPTER 30

When Salmon told McGee about his meeting with Banbury while they were riding back to the reservation McGee's reaction was at first sceptical.

'This guy Bilson could have wanted the whiskey for lots of reasons.'

'Such as?'

'Maybe he's holding a private party with, say, a couple of dozen guests. And he wants them all to have a good time.'

'With one hundred bottles of whiskey?'

'Yeah, well, maybe he wants to keep some of them for the next time he has a party.'

'There could be another explanation. Maybe he is going to supply them to the Indians so that they could start an uprising. After all, they haven't got over being beaten ten years ago.'

'What we've seen of them they certainly look to be a miserable bunch,' agreed McGee.

'If they rode into town after drinking whiskey, who knows what could happen?'

'They haven't got guns.' McGee pointed out. 'They've had to give up their weapons.'

'They've been allowed to keep their knives – so that they can hunt.'

'You don't have to tell me,' said McGee, touching his shoulder meaningfully.

'Well, anyhow, the evangelists might have noticed that something might be in the air,' said Salmon. 'We'll talk to them when we get to the reservation.'

They reached the reservation and found that the Children of God were rehearsing one of their hymns. They were singing the catchy hymn tune the two men had heard before.

I have decided to follow Jesus.
I have decided to follow Jesus.
I have decided to follow Jesus:
No turning back.
No turning back.

When they had finished Amy came across to greet them.

'Can we have a word with you and the other ladies?' asked McGee.

'Certainly.' She called them over.

When they were all seated on the grass, McGee

142

began: 'Have any of you noticed anything odd about the behaviour of the Indians in the past few days?'

His question was greeted by a collective shaking of heads.

'In what way?' demanded Flora.

'A friend of ours has been making some whiskey—'

'So we understand,' said Emma, drily.

'He's made a hundred bottles. He's sold them to a guy named Bilson. Nobody knows why Bilson wants the whiskey, but one theory is that he is going to supply the bottles to the Indians.'

'Oh, no!' There was a gasp of horror from several of the women.

'When is this going to happen?' demanded Amy.

'This guy Bilson collected the bottles this morning,' said McGee. 'So he's already got whiskey.'

'You say nobody knows him,' said Lizzie.

'That's right,' said Salmon. 'I was talking to the reporter of the *Caraton Gazette*. He said he didn't know him.'

'You two were in town when he collected the whiskey,' said Lizzie. 'One of you could at least have followed him to find out where he lived. Then maybe you could have found out more about him.'

'I wasn't with the whiskey supplier when they packed the bottles on to the cart.'

'You were, I suppose,' said Emma. She flung the accusation at McGee.

'Well . . . yes . . .' said McGee, sheepishly.

'I would have guessed,' snapped Emma.

'That doesn't help us with McGee's original question,' Amy pointed out.

'I haven't noticed anything different in the Indians' attitude,' said Flora. 'They hate us, and they will always hate us.'

'At least Petra has joined us,' said Amy. 'Have you noticed anything different in the braves' attitude?'

'What's attitude?' demanded Petra.

'Their behaviour. The way they are acting,' explained Amy.

'Well . . . maybe,' replied Petra.

'What do you mean?' demanded Lizzie.

'It's as if they are waiting for something.'

'A hundred bottles of whiskey,' said McGee.

'Oh, God! We'll all be raped in our tents,' shrieked Alice.

'Pull yourself together.' Her friend Lizzie seized her and shook her. 'We've just got to decide what we're going to do.'

'We'll put our heads together,' said Flora. 'We'll decide on the best course of action.'

'And we'll pray for guidance,' said Amy.

CHAPTER 31

McGee and Salmon's next visit was to the army camp. They were stopped at the gate, as usual, by two guards. McGee stated that they wanted to see the commanding officer on a mater of urgency.

'Aren't you the two guys who are staying in the Indian Reservation?' demanded one of the guards.

'That's right,' stated McGee.

'Right. You'd better come to see the lieutenant.'

He led them into the long wooden building. They passed through the bunk room where the beds on either side were neatly made. Salmon glanced at them enviously. They certainly looked more comfortable than the straw mattresses on which they had been sleeping during the past few nights.

They passed into another long room. Here there were several soldiers cleaning their rifles. They glanced up as McGee and Salmon went through. Some of them gave a friendly nod as they passed.

They were led into an office where the guard introduced them, then he was dismissed. The lieutenant seated behind the desk shook hands with them before waving them to the chairs.

'My name is Raleigh. No relation to the famous sailor, I'm afraid.' He was a young man still in his late twenties, with a pleasant, open face. 'I'm afraid the captain isn't here to see you. He's away on compassionate leave. He won't be back until tomorrow. I'm also afraid I can't offer you a drink of whiskey. It's one of the rules of the camp that there's no whiskey on the site.'

'It's about whiskey we've come to discuss,' said McGee.

He explained about the consignment of whiskey that Dan had completed. Surprise was stamped on Raleigh's face. When McGee had finished his explanation the lieutenant said: 'And you've no idea where that whiskey was delivered?'

'Unfortunately, no,' said McGee. 'If I'd thought about it I could have followed the wagon to find out its destination. But I didn't do it.'

The lieutenant put his fingers together and examined them. He was obviously deep in thought.

'And you say the evangelists haven't noticed anything unusual going on in the camp?'

'That doesn't mean to say that the Indians couldn't have hidden the whiskey in their tents,' said Salmon. 'There must be at least fifty tents on the reservation.'

'Seventy-two,' said the lieutenant, as though his mind was still on something else.

'If the Indians have got the whiskey, the chances are they'll drink it tonight,' said Salmon.

'Or early tomorrow morning,' stated McGee. 'Then they might go into town and God knows what might happen.'

'Yes, you could be right.' The lieutenant came to a decision. 'I'll post a couple of dozen of my men around the camp tonight. They will provide an early warning if there is any unusual activity in the Indians' tents.'

'The evangelists will be pleased to hear that,' said Salmon. 'They all thought they were going to get raped in their tents.'

Raleigh smiled. 'I don't think it will come to that. There is one thing you two can do, though.'

'What's that?' demanded McGee.

'Maybe you two can also keep watch tonight. If you see or hear anything unusual, fire a couple of shots. Our soldiers will come into the reservation to find out what's happening.'

'Yes, I think that will help the evangelists to sleep more safely in the beds,' said McGee.

The lieutenant stood up to show that the meet-

147

ing was over. 'It's nice to have two public-spirited guys like you on the reservation,' he said. As they were about to leave the way they had come the lieutenant said: 'You can come out through this door. It will save you going through the men's quarters.'

He opened a door which led into a small room. In it were stacked a few dozen rifles. There were also boxes of ammunition on the floor. He noticed the pair's interest in the guns.

'This is our armoury,' he said. 'Although we've never fired a shot in anger while I've been here.'

Back in the reservation McGee and Salmon explained to the evangelists the lieutenant's suggestion.

'We'll certainly all feel safer knowing that there are a couple of dozen extra soldiers keeping watch tonight,' said Flora.

'And that you two are keeping extra watch as well,' said Amy.

CHAPTER 32

McGee and Salmon tossed up to see who would take first watch. Salmon lost, so it was decided that he would keep watch from eleven until three. Then McGee would keep watch from three o'clock until dawn at seven o'clock.

Salmon took up his position outside the entrance to the tent. He was seated on a couple of thick bearskin rugs which were quite comfortable. But he had never quite mastered the technique of sitting cross-legged on them. He would manage for a short while, then he would find that his position would become uncomfortable. The result was he shifted his position dozens of times during his watch.

He heard nothing unusual. The reservation was as quiet as the proverbial grave. The only sounds were those of wild animals calling to each other in the hills. Normally he wouldn't have been able to

149

hear them, but in the stillness of the night the sounds carried. Mostly they were coyotes. But he thought he heard the occasional wolf. He shivered even though the night was warm.

At three o'clock he went inside to wake up McGee.

'Anything happening?' demanded McGee, as he donned his jacket.

'Nothing, so far.'

'Ah, well, let's hope we've got it all wrong. Maybe the whiskey was meant for a private party after all.'

McGee took up his post outside the tent. A couple of hours later he was smoking his fifth cigar and wondering idly where the soldiers were who were providing extra watchers. They must be stationed somewhere outside the reservation. They were probably smoking cigarettes or cigars too. It was funny the way cigarette smoke was more apparent at night. Or maybe it was just his imagination.

He wondered whether the soldiers who were stationed outside the camp could smell the smoke from his cigar. He certainly couldn't smell any smoke from their cigarettes.

Wait a minute! Suppose there weren't any soldiers. Suppose the lieutenant had gone back on his word to send them to keep watch on the reservation. Suppose there was only himself and Salmon to prevent what was going to happen tonight. Because in a blinding flash of realization he knew exactly what would be happening.

He dived inside the tent.

'Get your guns,' he shouted.

'Wha-at's happening?' demanded Salmon.

'We haven't a moment to lose.' He was still shouting.

Salmon grabbed his guns. He followed McGee, who was racing towards their horses.

They jumped on them in the rapid style they had often performed in the circus. Salmon followed McGee as he rode out of the reservation in a cloud of dust.

Luckily there was an almost full moon, so their horses were able to gallop without slackening their stride.

Salmon was confused. Why were they riding towards the town an hour or so before dawn? What were they hoping to find there? Had the Indians already begun to attack? They had been in the reservation all night and surely they would have spotted fifty or so braves leaving the place. However, he was prepared to follow McGee unquestioningly. He knew that McGee sometimes had these flashes of inspiration which turned out to be right more often than not.

Salmon was expecting them to carry on heading for Caraton, but to his surprise McGee swung to the left. Salmon followed him.

Where were they heading? There was only one answer. They must be heading towards the soldiers' camp. What were they going to do when they arrived there? Some of the soldiers were supposed to be watching the reservation. True, they hadn't spotted any as they rode out of the reservation. Also the two Indians who were always at the entrance to the reservation hadn't been there either. What was the significance of it? Had the Indians begun their attack? Not on the towns-folk, as expected, but on the soldiers? Surely they weren't stupid enough to tackle fully armed and trained soldiers. It would mean certain death for them.

Of course, many of the Indians believed that to die in battle was the most glorious thing that could happen to anybody. It would mean that they would become one with the Universal Spirit.

Wait a minute! If they were attacking the soldiers, surely by now there would be the sounds of gunfire? The soldiers wouldn't have just let themselves be attacked without retaliating. And they were now within half a mile or so of the camp. If the soldiers had fired at the Indians they would have heard the sounds of gunfire before now. But everything was as quiet as it had been all night.

They were now only a few yards away from the camp. Where were the guards who should have been on the gate? They weren't on duty either.

What was happening?

The answer was apparent when McGee swung into the compound. Salmon followed him. At the back entrance to the camp's main building stood a wagon. Its two horses were harnessed ready for it to move off. But it wasn't quite ready to move yet. Because three Indians were busy loading rifles and ammunition on to it.

Their surprise at seeing the new arrivals was stamped on their faces. It didn't survive long because McGee shot two of them and Salmon shot the other.

The sounds of the shots produced instant reaction. Three other Indians came out of the building. They were carrying bundles of rifles in their arms. They were in no position to argue when McGee said: 'Put your hands up.'

McGee jumped down from his horse. 'Keep an eye on these three,' he commanded.

He raced into the building. There were no Indians in the gun room. He dived through the door that led to the lieutenant's office.

The lieutenant had also been awakened by the sound of gunfire. He always left his lamp lit and so was able to see clearly the Indian who was in the room. He sat up in bed and reached for his gun. The Indian's reaction was quicker. He threw his knife which ended up in the lieutenant's heart.

At that moment McGee came into the room. He

took in the scene instantly. The Indian swung round to face him. But he wasn't armed and there was nothing he could do to defend himself against the man with the revolver.

McGee recognized the Indian. It was the one who had thrown the knife at him and almost killed him. McGee didn't hesitate. He shot the Indian in the heart.

The soldiers were beginning to stir. One of the sergeants came out from the bunk room.

'My friend is outside. He's captured three Indians. Relieve him of his duty,' snapped McGee.

More and more soldiers appeared, many of them only partly dressed. They filed sheepishly past McGee.

The sergeant returned, accompanied by Salmon.

'I don't know what to say . . .' he began.

'I suppose you're in charge now that the lieutenant is dead?' queried McGee.

'Yes, that's right.'

'And I suppose you're wondering whether this fiasco will be reported?'

'Yes.'

McGee turned to Salmon. 'What do you think?'

'The lieutenant is dead. Four of the Indians are dead. The other three Indians aren't going to advertise the fact that they tried to steal guns from the camp.'

'What about Bilson?' demanded McGee. 'He supplied the whiskey. Where will we find him?'

'I wouldn't know,' replied the sergeant. 'It was all arranged between the lieutenant and this guy Bilson. It was arranged so that we could have a drink while the captain was away.'

'The lieutenant was a fool, but he paid the price,' said Salmon.

'Of course, if there's an investigation, you two will have to stay around for a few weeks. These things take a long time to set up,' suggested the sergeant.

'I want to get back to the ranch,' stated Salmon.

'Of course, there might be a way out,' observed the sergeant.

'What do you suggest?' demanded McGee.

'If this is not reported then you two can go back home. It just happens that we didn't drink all of the whiskey Bilson brought here. We have at least a dozen bottles left. You'd be entitled to them for keeping quiet. Plus the men could hold a collection which I'm sure would be a useful contribution to your respective families.'

'Sergeant,' said McGee, 'you definitely deserve to become a lieutenant.'

CHAPTER 33

In the morning the two men packed up their few belongings. The Children of God had gathered to bid them farewell. They were singing one of their hymns.

Till we meet; till we meet;
Till we meet at Jesus' feet.
Till we meet again;
Till we meet again.
God be with you till we meet again.

All of the evangelists had tears in their eyes as they waved farewell to them. Emma was sobbing uncontrollably.

The pair swung their horses round and headed out through the gate. Salmon was wiping one eye as he rode along.

'I've got some dust in my eye,' he explained.

'You don't have to explain,' said McGee. He, too, was wiping an eye.

In Caraton they called at the bank. To their relief the $1,000 was there.

'If you will sign here,' said the manager. 'Just for the record.'

Their next call was to say farewell to Dan and Daisy.

Dan insisted on pouring them a drink.

'Just a small one,' said McGee. 'I don't want to go to sleep until we reach our first stop.'

'What's this about going to sleep?' asked an observant Dan.

'The whiskey you supplied to Bilson was intended for the soldiers in the camp. The idea was that they would drink your whiskey and while they were sleeping off the effects, the Indians would break into the camp and steal the guns. They would then use them to start an uprising.'

'Oh, no!' said Dan, aghast.

'Oh, my God!' exclaimed Daisy.

'Luckily McGee worked out where the whiskey had gone to,' said Salmon. 'And we were able to prevent the Indians' plan.'

'It was lucky,' said McGee. 'You see I spotted the wagon that Bilson used. You put the whiskey bottles in it yesterday. One of the shafts had been broken and then mended. I saw the same wagon outside the soldiers' camp when we called there later. At the time I didn't make the connection. But in the night it came to me.'

'McGee, you're a genius,' said Daisy, sitting on his lap.

'Even geniuses have to go home,' he said, gently disengaging himself from her.

'There are two men outside who are waiting to kill you.' Harold made the announcement as casually as though he had just stated that there were two people waiting for the stage. 'They've just put their guns under their coats,' he added.

McGee looked out through the window. Salmon joined him.

'It's the two men who killed Stone,' said McGee. 'The ones Ben described.'

'I'll take the one on the. left. You take the one on the right.'

McGee nodded to Dan, who gently eased the door open a fraction. The two men had their guns in their hands. Daisy closed her eyes. Another nod from McGee.

This time Dan flung open the door. The pair jumped down the steps. The sudden movement took Thorpe and Mallet by surprise. Before they could react by firing their own guns, McGee and Salmon had shot them.

Harold went over to confirm that they were dead. He nodded.

'We're not staying to fill in a form for the sheriff,' said McGee. 'We've got to get on our way.'

'I'll see the sheriff and explain what happened,' said Dan.

'There will be bounties on them,' said McGee. 'If you collect them, we'll come to Herford to pick them up.'

'That means I'll see you soon, McGee,' said Daisy, as they prepared to ride off.

They rode for several miles before either of them spoke.

'I've got a confession to make,' said Salmon. 'You know that gold nugget, I had from Ben.'

'Yes.'

'I gave mine to Clara, She saved my life by riding to tell you about my hanging. I just want to make sure that you don't mention it to Jill.'

'I've got a confession to make too,' stated McGee.

'What's that?'

'The gold nugget I had from Ben. I gave mine to Emma. She saved my life. Don't tell Letitia.'

When the pair of them digested the information they began to laugh. They were still laughing when Caraton disappeared from view behind them.